#notallbrendas

Still Alive

A novel

LJ Pemberton

Still Alive is a work of fiction. All of the characters, organizations, and events portrayed in this novel are products of the author's imagination or used fictitiously. Quotations for review/scholarly purposes that fall within fair use guidelines are welcome.

Cover design by Angelo Maneage

ISBN: 979-8-9874654-4-8

Published by Malarkey Books
Malarkeybooks.com

Printed in the United States of America

“What’s important isn’t the way in which reality constructs the characters’ consciousness, but rather the way in which the characters’ consciousness defines—and gives form—to reality.”

—*Ricardo Piglia, The Diaries of Emilio Renzi*

PART 1

1

We were all inside the house. All of us. Me, my brother, the babysitter, our father, our mother, our grandmother. Our grandmother was sleeping. She liked to sleep, and every time she went to her room to lie down I could tell she wanted most to be away from us, but right behind that she wanted to die. She had been here a long time. I think she thought if she laid down long enough maybe she wouldn't have to get up again. Mom had left that morning to run some errands, which was her way of saying she was going to go fuck Brenda's husband. I always hated that name, Brenda. It sounded too much like Rhonda, which was a name I hated too. You couldn't make much of yourself with a name like that. You'd just end up melting American cheese for pasta over a gas burner, praying for next year to be better, while in the next room your son rubbed one out for the third time since getting home from school. Anyway, mom was back now, and dad was in the living room asleep on the couch with his hand stuck in the waistband of his pants. My brother was on the phone probably claiming he wasn't racist because his girlfriend was Black. He loved to do that, as though a girl could ever rescue him or anyone from the ugliest thing inside them. The babysitter was there to watch me, and even though I'm sure she had a name, I don't remember it now. Let's call her Jen. That's a good generic white girl name and in pre-hip Portland, in 1989, it was as ubiquitous as Radio Shacks and boredom.

My brother was the first out the door after we heard the crash. I should mention his name was James then, although he changed it in 2004 after he found enlightenment at an ashram. For a while I called him Richard Gere because I didn't care enough to remember what he changed it to, but back then he was James, and it's good you know that because the next thing that happened was dad startling up and yelling, James, where you going?

He was going to the yard, where the crash had happened, and so was I. Jen followed suit. What was she even doing there? Oh yeah. They were paying her to take me to swimming lessons at the local Y. My parents were really good at outsourcing the most annoying parts of parenting. But anyway, it was James and Jen and me and I saw the man's head first, his mouth agape on the lawn, right next to the mangled metal and plastic and glass that had been a Nissan coupe about five minutes before. Jen puked. James stood there, still high, and I wasn't sure if he cared and I suddenly understood why he liked smoking so much. Dad came out, then mom. Gran slept through the whole thing. Later I'd hear mom telling her the paramedics couldn't have done anything, his head came clear off, and she would have delight in her voice, and excitement—the first I'd heard in years.

Of course, I walked up to the head. It didn't yet matter that it had a body or a name. I was seven and I felt the way I did about most things I had never seen before—I was curious. There was a blood spatter in the short October grass and his eyes stared at the bushes behind me. I laid down in front of him. His mouth was open and his tongue relaxed. He had pale skin and brown hair, cut into the side part of a good accountant. It was evident he clipped his ear hairs. I decided he must have been old enough to have a kid my age and then I wondered who else was in the car, or cars, I should say, because there were two, or had been two, and dad was standing by the window of one of them, staring at the rest of the man's body.

Michael, jesus, get V away from there, I heard my mom say, and then I heard her talking to 911, and telling them what had happened. I got away from where dad was so that I could see in the other car, and there I saw a woman and a man, still alive, but stuck where they were. They're still alive, I said, and I heard mom say oh dear god and then she told 911 and dad came over and tried to pry on the door but there was no moving it. They'd have to use the jaws of life. The woman turned her head to look at me and I saw her eyes focus for a minute before looking then at something else, and then not looking at anything anymore. Nevermind, I whispered, but then I remembered that the man beside her might still be alive. They were both dressed up, like they had been going somewhere important, but later we found out they were Seventh Day Adventists and had just been coming home from church.

For a full three minutes I wanted to keep the head. I thought about it, still in the grass, while I watched the paramedics pry the man from the Ford his wife had died in. V, go inside, I heard my mother say, but I was unwilling, and my father was trying to be useful and getting in the way. Jen was gone. No swim lessons today. James had called me a tiny sicko and then retreated inside. It was better than calling me Blank, his more common nickname for my silence. I walked back to my room and pulled out my diary. (I still have it.) That entry says: There was a car accident in the yard. I saw a man's head in the grass because his body was still in his car. A woman in the other car died too, but her husband didn't. (I don't think.) James is a jerk.

It wasn't the first car accident that had happened near our house, but it was the first that had jumped the curb and landed where we couldn't ignore it. Fender benders were to be expected. Our wood-paneled ranch sat at the intersection of a five-way stop with three stop signs and two blind pullouts. Later we'd learn that the man who died had been drinking. Later we'd learn he had tried to rob a 7-11 at two in the afternoon. Later we'd learn he wasn't an accountant at all, just a boring small-time criminal with a moneyed face. In high school, I sat on the steps of that house and told Kristen about that afternoon and she'd smoked a cigarette and crossed her hands over her knees and said I must be pretty fucked up. I tried to kiss her after that and she burned her cigarette into my arm. We didn't talk again.

Over the years, I've collected other skulls. A squirrel skull I found sun bleached in a field next to wind-blown bits of fur on its maggoty body. A cat skull from neighborhood road kill. My prize is the raccoon skull I found half stripped on a trail in North Carolina. Leroy was with me and he was chanting incantations to the trees as we walked. He's as close to a wizard as a real person can be, which only means he can make you believe the earth has a language you could speak if you were humble enough to learn. When we are together it feels as though our lives don't carry the residue of any past. He's an other-brother. A brother who does not find me mad, who does not interpret my silence as a void or my speaking as a totality.

Beck asks me what, asks me what the silence is. What it contains. I just smile. It is easier that way. It is easier than saying I am thinking about that time I fucked Daniel on the couch still in my red dress. Or when I kissed Annie in bed after we danced in a poet's living room like we could make the known new with our lust. Beck has red hair, white skin. She's got that ethereal wood-goddess thing going for her that the white supremacists really like. Her skin gets goosebumps when I touch her. Gere thinks I must be showing off, as if there was something less true about how I want Annie or Beck than how I wanted Jarrett or Daniel before them. And the others. As if any desire could be less true than another.

I call up Leroy and say let's go to the house. He asks if it's the anniversary and I say, naw, last week, but you know I was working. Let's go on Saturday. He says he's in. We get up at 5 a.m. and drink Rockstars to get our blood pumping while we listen to Daft Punk before dawn, the rhythm pounding heartbeatrollingbeatroll, until we're there and I'm standing in the yard like the ghost I always thought should have been. He doesn't ask why I return some years and not others—he just stands beside me when I do. This year I hold his hand. He's got his thumb through his hoodie sleeve and the edge of it is thick against my palm. I come back because I think whatever I've become started in that yard, with that head in the grass. Leroy got his feet somewhere in the woods of Pennsylvania, wandering through human and animal habitats with those surgeon's eyes of his. We came out parallel. Whatever holds two people across time and distances, we carry for each other. Für dich, mi amour.

That night we're on instant messenger and he's stoned and watching the Trinity Broadcast Network, cracking up about the eschatologists so hard I can almost hear his cackling through the broadband. Look, there's a lot we don't know about the unseen, I say. And clearly Jack Van Impe does, he says. We call Impe's wife Mrs. Skeletor and he says I should come with him to this basement punk show on the East Side. He asks if I'm bringing Beck and I say we ain't like that yet. I roll up in my cowboy boots and hoodie with my hair down like Brigitte Bardot and he tosses his cigarette. We walk in together. The basement is somehow both hot and that cold-damp that only concrete rooms can be. Overfull. Eight years later I'll get the same feeling standing sentinel at Cake Shop in the LES, but this was Portland, Oregon, circa 2003. Back when we believed things like hardcore and straightedge could still be taken seriously. Back when all you needed to eat, sleep, or drink was a few gigs or some basic daytime racket. Rent was cheap.

We don't dance so much as hang by the walls. The music is so loud you can't hear more than a chordbeat but the singer is selling it like he might die tonight and everyone else is ready no matter what.

They're bumping and jumping and knocking against each other, human pinball bowling pins in hand-me-downs and safety pins. We make eye contact when we see something worth seeing and make eye contact when we hate something that's just been done. I knock his shoulder during the encore because this soft butch just walked in with a shaved head and mexibrows I could spend three decades figuring out. He leans over and whispers conspiracies and then kisses me on the cheek. I scoot off the wall I've been propping myself up on and sidle next to her with my hands in my pockets and my eyes on the table of red cups and juju juice in the back. When she doesn't make any moves, I get a cup for myself and then sip on it, back on the wall, nodding my head with the music and then staring at her until she glances back. It's a glance like a sly cat and I grin with my cup clenched between my teeth. Eyes stuck on each other but still both shy. This is the first hello.

Leroy comes over and I hand him my cup. I'm still facing her. She's facing the band. There are other people around but they don't matter. Leroy kicks at my foot and then gestures with his chin like I should go over there. I lean over and whisper in his ear, naw she'll come, and she does, when the encore is over and the people who don't matter start leaving in packs and singles through the basement door to the drizzle outside. She says, I saw you staring, and I say, I saw you come in. She bites her lip. I say this is Leroy, and Leroy shakes her hand and says, I gotta see about a boy like he's the first person to ever make fun of *Good Will Hunting.* I crack up and we knock elbows because we do that instead of shake hands sometimes and she hangs by.

I want a burger, I say, like it's an invitation, and she gets it, and so we walk out to my beat-to-shit nineties blue civic. She's got on a long-sleeve black tshirt and mustard Carhartt pants. I can tell her tits are small and her arms are built. Already I wish we were having brunch three weeks later like it might become a habit so I can get these butterflies out of my stomach. Black eyes. I order coffee and a cheeseburger at the diner and she orders a cappuccino and a piece of apple pie a-la-mode. We're waiting and she says her name is Lex. The x trips off like every other name is lacking without it. Virginia, I say, but most people call me V, I say, and she nods, puts her napkin in her lap. Then we're off—covering all of it, where she was born (Manhattan) what she's been up to (painting, hustling, bartending) and the same for me (Hillsdale) (temping and writing). The future doesn't exist. I'm already lost and the coffee is in its second cup. Three hours later we're naked in my bed and I'm wondering if she'll come under or over me.

It's frozen, that first breath when we were slow undressing, and I was sitting straddle, our bras removed, our breasts caressing the other's as we embraced, I with my fingers running through her hair and her, with her mouth on my neck, then my collar, then my nipple, and then we were on the bed, our hands reaching for that warm home between each other's legs. I put my hand on her chin and for a moment, paused, looked at her—those eyes, coy. No ice. Just paused, held in the balance, like I could reach out and catch it even now if I willed it. The first exhale, released like a gift. She let it sit between us—I'll call it desire—and we kissed beyond it, around it, preserved that breath in the morning, left it to grow in the months that followed.

On the phone with James that December he asks if I'm bringing my hot dyke home and I tell him we're leaving town for Christmas. We go to Vancouver—the Canadian one. I forget my name when we're together. She keeps her hands in her pockets, arms straight, and I knit my hands into the space between her elbow and side, clasping with intention. Who owns who? Our affections bleed like our sex. In a cold alley she kisses me against a wall. I don't care that she hardly speaks. I am in love with the idea of her, as if I could interpret color, as if her urgency meant more than insecurity. She pulls my hair. I burn.

Mom calls me and I can hear her smoking a cigarette. She says she's glad I'm happy. I can hear the self-congratulation in her voice, as if being an approving mom to her queer kid makes her worthy of a Nobel. She's talking about this new guy who's definitely the one. (They're all definitely the one, and most are definitely gone when she gets bored seven months later.) I think I'm just glad dad's too busy with his own life to notice. Not because he still cares, but because he wouldn't do well knowing her love for him might have been as shallow.

Lex moves in. She starts paying rent after three months when she lands a gallery space in Northeast and sells five paintings to a rich bitch in the West Hills.

Fancied herself a patron, Lex laughs, when we go out that night. Patrons come pretty cheap these days, I say. Like swingers, she says. I love her meanness. I envy her self-containment. News from my work-study job lacks the glamour of her failures and successes. She says I could have a piece of the excitement if I submitted more, but I'm bad at knowing where to send what or even believing anyone wants to read what I write anyway. I'm more full of words than I am of ambition; besides, I need to graduate. I know she doesn't care because she needs something steady to keep going. I'm insurance against the flood.

We're dancing by the jukebox, too close to it, each other, and Leroy shows up. He never announces himself, just arrives, and I find him. Where's K? I ask, and he says they broke up. He says he moved his shit out in the middle of the night when K got drunk and thought it was a good look to wake the neighbors breaking shit on the floor, temper-tantrumming between shots like Leroy had any answer for his frustrations. People are so fucking predictable, says Leroy. He is right, but he is lying. He loved K for his instability. That apartment was shit, anyway, I say. He nods. He's crashing with a neighbor. He's got a line on a room closer to us on Clinton in southeast. We get up to bounce to the Fez and Lex closes the tab. My turn, she says, and then wraps her arm around the back of me as we walk towards Leroy's car. I'm buzzed and we're making out in the back seat past the night signs, Leroy's cig smoke blowing back to my nostrils from his cracked window. When we get there, Lex slaps the bouncer's ass like he owes her something and we get in, no cover. I should be used to this, but I never seem to get a handle on who Lex knows, where's she been. She doesn't lie, but her days are full of secret hours, withheld, unshared. Leroy pulls me onto the dance floor and we slip in and out of our skin with the projected videos and blue-black lowlight of the thrumming room. When the strobe comes on, he is Dionysius and I am wine. We get lost in ourselves and I don't feel guilty because Lex is also lost, somewhere away from me, and blitzed on coke when she returns.

She sidles up to my hip and then I see Beck on a side couch cozied up with a dude. Beck's sucking on a lollipop and when she looks over, we lock eyes. She pulls the lolli out and I keep my stare. I can feel Lex against me and I know Beck knows what she sees just like I know what I'm looking at. Beck breaks out in a big smile and then blows me a kiss across the room. I wink. That's that then. Later I see her making out with that guy. Maybe they left together. Maybe Beck left him alone. She does what she wants. So do we. Me, Lex, and Leroy roll out for waffles after 2 a.m. The sun comes up. I go to sleep old and wake up younger.

We bent time like tesseracts back then, rolling around and through different places and ages like costumes we could try on and discard. Lex acted like one of those rock stars too wired to make it past twenty-seven. She'd paint in ratted-up jeans and then finger fuck me on the concrete floor of her studio. We made dinner out of spare change—cheese, some bread, leftover beer in the fridge. What else could we be? Stability was a myth.

One night when we were looking for rolling papers to make a spliff she found a pic of my grandmother in a desk drawer. Who's this old lez, she said. You think? I said. She squinted and stared: Coulda been. Who knows? I said. I put the picture away. It was my grandmother, I said. Dad's mom. Hot bitch, she smiled. When she was young? No doubt, I said. I rifled in the desk and inhaled the memory of her body, still, on the bed. She died like she wanted—took a nap, never woke up. I found her stiff. Dad said, well then. Mom called the morgue. James was already gone—waiting tables somewhere in Colorado—not interested enough to come home. They put her in the ground on a Sunday and it was the first time I ever wore a dress. I know she wasn't happy, I said. Who is? said Lex, with that casual relationship she has always had to pain.

God those first years I could drink her cynicism up, so bright and shiny was I on my own, so eager to imbibe the sharp crackle of her disdain. She made me believe fuckups could be as precious as children. That any ordinary day could be special. There was poetry in the way she carried groceries from the store. There was meaning in the way she ignored responsibility. I wanted her. I wanted to be her.

I barely knew myself.

We ranted against the Iraq War. We kissed each other in Pioneer Square in front of evangelical street prophets. We gave money to camo-clad kids and their dogs, holed up under awnings. We believed in righteousness, in the power of our love to change the world. I stumbled with her in the rain after a late night at the Shanghai Tunnel and I said she was my starboi and we went home and fucked in the living room of my one-bedroom apartment because it seemed better to do it there, somehow more desperate and more alive.

It's late summer and Leroy and I go driving on a Saturday, just the two of us, and we decide on a loop through the Eastern Oregon wilds. There: fossils in the ground and wide amber hills beneath blue sky. The occasional wind turbine. We pass rivers and stop for gas. Near a tucked-in ghost town we see a herd of pronghorn antelope grazing, and then a child, and more children, running towards leftover lean-tos of the pioneer past. Someone lives here. They stare at us as we roll through, our hopes of trespassing and exploration dashed by their wide eyes and the knowledge that there are adults behind the closed windows. The kind we wouldn't want to meet. We drive on.

I hate my job, I tell him. At least you can pay your bills, he says. His gig pumping gas eats his hours but never pays quite enough to stop juggling food and electric, gas and insurance. We stop by a lake and skinny dip to cool off, leaning on driftwood when we get tired of treading water. He tells me a story about the time he found a dog carcass in the back yard of the farmhouse he grew up in. Pieces of hair were strung across the ground, dry and matted, and he thought it was a woman's hair, before he saw the skull. On the drive home, the sun begins to dip and turn the hills into angled shadows, and I see three wolves running across their slant terrain. We pull over and watch them, before rejoining the road home. I kiss him when he drops me off and Lex asks me how it was out there. There are people living in the ghost towns, I tell her. Did you see them? she asks. We saw their children, I say. Later that night, when we're sweaty and laying around in a post-orgasmic haze, I turn over on my stomach and tell her we saw wolves. You're magical, she says, and traces the hairline on my forehead.

She is gone the next morning, before I wake up. This is common on Sundays but I am still nervous with her absence. I know she is at the studio, but I miss her lazing with me like in early days. I get selfish and buy coffee and show up, believing I am always a good surprise. She tries to give me the reaction I want, but I can hear the hurry in her voice and the annoyance at my presumption. I ask her how it's going and she says pretty good. She's says she's still hung up on where the big piece is going and we both know she's talking about the ten-foot canvas she framed herself and started painting a year before. It leans against a wall behind us with a smattering of blue and green blending together like a still wave. It looks angry, despite the cool colors, and I hate that I am not enough to satisfy her. V, you've got to find your own mission, she says to me, and I know this is her way of saying I shouldn't have come. Don't patronize me, I say, and I take my coffee and my bag and leave.

She's terse over dinner and we go to sleep in the same bed but not together. I get up the next morning and go to work in my usual black bland costume of business casual whatever and try to put it out of my mind. B, Jabba the Hutt's assistant, is nose to the grindstone before I come in the door. Coffee's ready, she says, and I say thanks, before making myself a cup and putting in my headphones. One more day, click-monkeying my way through another schedule, another customer call, another file system. Jabba comes in with a bag of Burger King breakfast and that privileged grin of his. V, looks great, he says (what does?), and I resent his praise. It's like hearing him thumb through a business book on good management while he takes a shit in the single stall. I nod and hope that'll do. Fuck. I text Leroy. He's at the gas station smoking weed and reading

Hegel between pumps. Then I think about Gere over in India, sitting on his ass praying and eating lentils. I hate him for his exit strategy. He'd say I hate him because I want to. I'd say hate is useful.

James sends his love from Rishikesh, Mom chimes. She's called to catch up. It's another Saturday morning. I will listen to her sobbing, and then go for a drive, hiding in the rolling beat of some new electronica or this hangover I want to keep because it gives me an excuse not to speak. I am here, I want to say, and I am drowning. Yes, he is so good to always send his love, I say. Your father is marrying Daniela, she says. Then I hear the ice in the glass and the drawling slur. I know, I say. What I do not say: the invitation is on the fridge. What I do not say: Lex and I are going and I already picked out my suit. So instead I change the subject because mom won't ever get better if I don't change the subject, right? Right? Can I change mine?

Lex, lex, lex.

We wanted to mindfuck some of the heteros at dad's wedding so Lex wore the dress with her shaved head and I had big Texas hair with my blue pantsuit. Do you Michael take Daniela? said the preacher, and I sat still in the white folding chairs beside the sea, staring at the rolling waves. Lex was on her phone because some gallery in Massachusetts had gotten interested in her stuff and the curator was texting random questions just to keep her on the hook until they finalized terms. Daniela looked like the kind of girl I would have wanted to know had she not been my future step-person: ambitious and femmey, with that second-generation immigrant determination that always made me hate myself for my self-pity. Her nails were flawless. They shoved cake in each other's mouths and we made people feel good about loving gay people by giving them the right kind of smiles when they asked: and how long have you two been together?

Eighteen months. One year, six months. However you want to count it. That night we went back to the hotel and put on pjs and watched tv for a while before clicking it off and talking in the dark. I don't think I believe in marriage, she said. I had my head on her shoulder and her arm was holding me against her. I could smell her breath, liquored and thirsty. What does it mean when people say that? I said. I wanted her to do better. I expected better than a phrase I'd heard in the mouths of other people with lesser intellects, always so sure of their originality, always so cliché in their reasoning. You never let things be, she said. No, I said, I guess not. We were quiet and she reached and ran her free hand on my forearm, stacked on her waist. We were close, closer than fucking it seemed, and she was thinking and I was waiting. It was heaven's hell. I don't think I want my fate dependent on anyone else, she said. And does marriage make that true? I asked. I don't know, she said. More likely.

I didn't want to have this conversation. I resented that one possibility could suddenly be yanked from my options. Marriage wasn't even legal yet, then. But it hung over us like a prize, like a dream we fancied we could judge better, for the distance of it. Don't all relationships do that though? I asked. And she was quiet. We fell asleep in her non-response and woke up with it between us.

She left me in the morning three weeks later. The day was beautiful, because it was June, and I was sad.

2

We were all inside the house. Two years after the crash. Mom wore her red house dress with stars embroidered on the shoulder. It looked like a costume from another era, and it made her more beautiful than she was, as though the right outfit might conjure up an elegant almost-Dietrich from the mousy brown of her hair. Dad had her in his broad denim lap and I didn't mean to see them—it was so unlike them to touch each other—but she was close to him and he was smiling. There were martini glasses beside them. I came around the corner from the hall and stopped with my school calendar in hand. It was the first time I had ever seen them as two adults, and I was just a stranger in their house, with no more right to their attention than an audience member to two actors on a stage. Then James screamed from his bedroom that he needed thirty bucks for drama club even though I knew half of that was a down payment on his next eighth. Mom looked up and she saw me seeing her and I ran back to my room and closed the door. I thought, maybe, she would come down the hall and knock and she would ask what I wanted, but she didn't, and I was alone with my new knowledge in the quiet of my bedroom.

Leroy asks me if I've heard anything. We are in bed together, but we have not been fucking and aren't thinking we would. It was easier to be close, like this, when we were lonely, than give up on love. She's been hooking up with Beck, he says, and I say I don't care, look, it's not like it's a big community, and he says okay. What have you been reading, I ask, and I prop my head up on my arm, and he says he has been reading these old gnostic texts—Pistis Sophia, he says, and the Hypostasis of the Archons.

I listen as he tells me about them, about how the Hypostasis is a midrash of the creation story where Eve has the breath of Sophia and Adam has only the breath of Yahweh. He laughs: Yahweh thinks he is the only god, isn't that perfect? And I smile and he tells me that Adam rapes Eve because he wants to possess the Sophia in her—but Sophia leaves, her spirit leaves, he says, and becomes the tree of life. There's more, he says, but that tree's my favorite part. I want to be a tree, I say. He kisses me. Sophia, he says, you're so much more than a tree. What do you know about trees? I say. More than most people, he says. We pull the covers up. The sun has set and the room has slowly darkened except for the light beside my bed. I wait. I tell myself that life is long and I have to be okay with waiting, and then he rolls to me and asks if I remember Philip?

Philip who looks like he was chubby in high school? I ask. Philip who loves Isherwood and who flirts with us both, he says. Have you been in touch? I ask. They have. Two hours later we are at Holocene dancing beneath neon lights and Leroy is edging up closer to Philip and I am twirling and when I stop I see Leroy's smiling eyes. The room is crowded and the lights are blue and pink and red and purple and gold and they're swirling over us and around us and flashing off the disco ball hanging over our heads. I'm in love with the noise, with my feet, with my spinning body, my kicking legs, my shaking hair.

Leroy's dancing beside me and Philip is getting looser, letting his shoulders drop, realizing it's okay to do this, it's okay to like us both, it's okayyyyyy—and then I stop, really stop, because beyond the crowd, against the wall, I see Lex. She's sitting next to a thin woman, a woman like I'll never be, whose small tits are peaking through shreds in her oversized black tshirt. I pretend I haven't seen them. I pretend I haven't seen those small nipples. I leave the group, leave the floor completely, and get a standing spot at the bar. Order a g&t. A woman puts her hand on the small of my back and I smile and she asks me my name and I tell her. She says something about how she moved here three months ago from Wisconsin, and I say that Portland's an alright place if it's what you're looking for, and she keeps talking and I'm not listening. I'm still looking at Lex without actually looking over at her. My face is inches from this Wisconsin woman's mouth, and I'm trying to care, but I've seen her—I've seen Lex. I say I'm sorry. I tell Wisconsin I think I need to be alone right now, and thankfully, she leaves. A little huffy. Who cares? I sip my gin and bounce my head. I do that club thing where you're busy even though you're not doing anything. Nothing at all. In the middle of the dance floor a group of deaf friends are dancing and laughing and signing in exaggerated articulation. The beat bass beat vibrates the floor beneath them, beneath me, in the wall, all around us. I sip again, and then spot Leroy with Philip, and I watch Philip flirting with his own gay self as much as he is flirting with Leroy. Lex hasn't seen me. It is better this way. She's got her head back and she's watching the thin woman's clavicle and the gin and music and distance and lights erase what I know about discretion. I stare. My vision blurs and then focuses and then blurs again. I wish-want them both, imagine myself between them, try to turn away, fail, sip, and order myself to believe it's a good thing I don't always get what I want. I finish the last cold dregs, leave my glass at the bar, and rejoin Leroy and Philip to dance.

The music thumps and soars and the three of us gyrate and smile together and not together in different configurations. When we line up, our pelvises play chicken with touch—up and down and around—and the music continues, always the music. I yell over Philip's shoulder in the din, yell to Leroy that I'm going to kiss him, and Leroy knows that I mean Philip and Philip knows that I mean Philip, and Leroy responds: my dear, if you do, you kiss him for us both. So I do. Philip's mouth is small and the kiss is wet and fine and good and then Leroy turns Philip's head and kisses him too, longer, while I brush Philip's hair from his eyes and run my hand slowly down his back. He shivers. He is beautiful between us, so fresh in new knowledge, and I am watching the veins on his neck stand from his skin so that I will not look in another direction. They take a breath and then I kiss Leroy, long, longer this time, and he understands. I pull away and look at him and he smiles at me and I tell him: I'm gonna go take a walk, and he says, I'll see you tomorrow? and I say yes and I leave.

My mother's apartment living room is hot and she is single again. You can't trust this fucking town, she says, before dinner. The roses grow like weeds. I am wishing I was by the river and it was morning. I am wishing the season would change. She has made filo bowls with rib tips—an attempt at what she calls "country living"—but it is only the two of us and I am tired of only. Your brother has decided to stay at the ashram permanently, she says, and I say, that's interesting. (I don't know how he'd have the money, or why he should be so lucky, or if he even knows what the concept of permanent is—but she is discreet about any support and doesn't flinch.) She pours a butter sauce on the asparagus. She opens two bottles of wine. The Basement Pub has trivia tonight, I say, and she says I can walk—it isn't that far anyway—and I don't have a good excuse to argue with her. I will enjoy what I can.

I'm not going to ask about your father, she says, which is her way of reminding me that she wants to know more but knows that she isn't supposed to say so. There isn't anything to tell anyway, I say. He has moved on, I don't add. Why do you still care? I don't ask. Then, aloud: what did you imagine for your life when you were my age? That's a cruel question, she says. She holds her knife blade down with one finger extended over the blunt edge as she strips a rib of its meat. I watch the precise movements of her hands for clues, to know the shape of her anxiety, why she treats men like a habit and why she believes alcohol is good for anything. Of course I learn nothing; only gamblers carry secrets in their hands. The wine makes me hot. I get up for a glass of water and I hate her as she feels sorry for herself.

She pours more wine. The conversation does not get better. She tells me I'm so much like her mother, it depresses her. You invited me to dinner, I say. I did, she says. It does not help. I do my dishes and leave; in the night air my hands remember the scalding water and the hair stands alert and awful—so dry and itchy as I walk west. The pub is crowded when I get there and I don't feel like texting up a team. I turn and head into one of the expensive neighborhoods and duck into a café for some coffee and pie. It's quiet. A few college students sit in the corner studying for their futures and I stare out the window at the oasis of grass where on other days, fun-lovers have gathered for croquet. I wonder if they know something I do not—the nature of life, the goodness of a good crew. The city is killing me. There is nothing for me here but sex and rain.

At home I turn my cat skull to face me from the top of my dresser. It watches me as I sleep, dress, get my next gig in the Pearl District, grow my hair out, smile again when the sun peeks through, finally, and I bring home a chess player—his name so common it takes me three weeks to remember. I avoid saying it during sex, afraid I'll grab the wrong one. Matthew, but Matt to his coworkers, he says. It is an attempt at uniqueness. I don't disabuse him. He bikes everywhere and has four zombie escape plans. I am bored, but he has decent taste in movies. We watch Scorsese together (the bad ones) and I keep suggesting Tarkovsky but he prefers the French new wave. He finds a slip of paper by my desk with a note I'd written down, drunk, as a reminder: do not text Lex. Who's Lex? he asks.

My ex, I say. Are you still in love with him? He asks. Her, I say. Oh, he says and forgets he was waiting for more of an answer.

I ghosted or he did. I don't remember now. In the wet spring I filled the time with new ambitions. I burned my hands on the stove and killed pallets of plants. I dyed my hair blonde, decided I didn't look like myself and dyed it back. Afternoons passed at other people's bbqs. I drank wine, fell asleep, told stories, got lost in the woods, paid my rent—barely. Leroy and I went to the porn shop and bought salvia. We smoked it and laid around on blankets in the dark and waited for something to happen. On the weekend we went to the mortuary and read the names and epitaphs, imagined the grudges of the dead and wondered what secrets they had taken with them. Other afternoons we went to Movie Madness and held up titles and play-acted their best-of until we settled on Camus' *Black Orpheus* and Will Vinton's claymation *The Adventures of Mark Twain.* Strangers auditioned to be our lovers.

One night I smoked so much weed I started narrating the narration and then I fell asleep on the couch in the basement, with Leroy snoring in his bed a few feet away, hidden behind green and purple batiks that passed for walls. The next morning Leroy said it was okay that nothing made sense right now, that I was figuring out my drag name, my flavor. I told him I could see the point of cannibalism, but I knew I wasn't supposed to say so. He said the taboo around eating people was relatively recent, actually. I decided my flavor was lime. Leroy said I was too sincere for drag, and I did not argue.

She had seen me, but in the intervening months between when I watched her at the club and the morning she texted me as I dressed for an admin gig out past 84th Street, I had not known. Weeks, the same: sleep, wake, shower, coffee, work, shower, rest, sleep and again. Still, I had carried the memory of that night in my pocket like a rock plucked from a mountain. In my boredom I had rolled it in my fingers. In the sun I had held it up and stared at the lines of quartz, wondered at what was inside. I looked at my phone. Her words: I'd like to talk next time we run into each other. Coffee? she asked. Yes? I thought, yes? I wanted to think of another answer but I couldn't, and so I texted yes (she had seen me?), and we met, and it was summer, again, in Portland with the sun high in the evening. No wind. I wore harness boots to feel tall and a jacket to feel hidden. She arrived late, with a nod, and slid into the booth in front of me. She chose Dot's because she knew I was a sucker for burritos, and (this was before the smoking ban) the darkness and the velvet paintings and the smoke made it feel like rules were for other people.

Coffee and a beer. Two beers. She drank the coffee fast and the beers slow, nursed between her lips, between her words. How've you been, she asked me, and I said I keep going, and she said this summer is pretty nice so far, and then she said I fucking miss you. I sipped my beer. (You know I wanted to hear it, but I didn't know what to do with it once I did.) I said I missed some things about us, and then she got into what happened after us, and half of it was answers I had wanted to hear months ago, but what good was that to me now?

You know I thought about calling you, she said (but she didn't call), and I nodded and watched for the plate that might have my burrito on it and not the couple's across the way. I just don't think I'm good at being responsible for anyone, she said, and I said, what the hell are you talking about? And my burrito came and she said, you seemed like you wanted so much (and I fucking did), and I said: I wanted you to see me as your equal.

It wasn't a lie, but it wasn't all true, because that was what I wanted now, not then. Then, I didn't care. Then, I just wanted her. She unzipped her light hoodie and I saw she was wearing a ribbed tank over her bound breasts, her stomach so tight beneath them. She leaned forward. I'm afraid, she said, and what little ground I was standing on gave way. I leaned in. Managed somehow not to say: me too. I feel like I'm gonna unravel, she said, or need to? Too tight or something. You're not a fucking ball of yarn, I whispered. No, no, you're right, she said, and smiled all wry and then reached and picked a piece of tomato off my plate and popped it into her mouth. She knew I was back. An hour later we were walking side by side to my place and then we were standing in front of my duplex and she had her hands in her pockets and then she didn't—one finger was tracing from my collarbone to the topmost button of my shirt. She unbuttoned it and then took her hand away and I stood in front of her, rapt, breathing more heavily now, my chest nearly exposed to the street, to passersby.

The problem is I like your games, I said. I know you do, she said. And I did. I loved them. I loved her power trips and disappearances. I wanted to be found and lost and found again. I didn't care about not getting hurt—I'd been hurt and come out okay. I believed I could do it again.

We were together and not. We did not text except to meet. We did not meet except to fuck. Our dalliances were punctuated by total silence between meetings. We were without the regular hindrances: we did not discuss family. We did not plan. When we were together, we spoke of daydreams and let our ordinary anything belong to another time. She told me she had been reading Kant. She told me she had been reading Augustine. I said I had an ongoing flirtation with Marx. She slipped her fingers in my underwear and said it was because I was red inside. I sneered at her bad joke. She bit my lip. I licked her lips. We lost hours and forgot our names. I bought her a cross and she hung it upside down over her mirror—like Peter's, she said, as the good lapsed-

Catholic she was, and we were in the bathroom, getting ready to go somewhere—out? Did it matter? I was already dressed. She was shirtless, with her binder tight around her chest. Hear my confession, I said. She spit out her toothpaste. What do you have to confess, she said, putting my hair behind my ear with her finger, bringing her face so close I could smell the mint on her breath. Forgive me, father, for I have sinned, I said. I was just this side of a laugh, but I wanted it to roll; I wanted her to play. Tell me, my child, she said and moved closer, kissing my neck with my head cradled in her hand. How have you sinned? she asked. I was pinned against the sink, back to the mirror. I dropped the lipstick in my hand. I have coveted that which is not mine, I said. Have you? she asked and she pulled my shirt over the top of my head and hands. Do you know your hail mary? she asked, and she ran her finger down my back, unharnessing my bra and then cupping my breasts in her hands. I know the beginning, I whispered, and she nodded and I began: Hail Mary, full of grace. She answered: the Lord is with thee, and my chest heaved against her strong fingers. Blessed art thou amongst women, she breathed, her mouth an inch from my nipple, and blessed, she licked, is the fruit of thy womb. Jesus, I exhaled, and she took me in her mouth and said yes between her teeth, my left nipple bit between them.

We did not last long, but our fucking sustained me through boring dates and the gray slide into fall. Jobs came and went. Time slowed. When the Cuban welder next door—Ernesto—invited me inside for a smoke one evening, I felt reckless and said yes. I sat on his couch and smoked his weed and loved his laugh. He said he loved my name, that it reminded him of his mother. He showed me his scars. He begged me to stay. I went home and touched myself to the thought of him fucking me, but then the thought was her, or she was him, but it was Lex, only Lex, no matter how it began.

Later he sees me going out and asks: you have a new boyfriend? Something like that, I say. You are a heartbreaker, he says, too many secrets. I don't mean to keep secrets, I say. No? he asks. What is there to tell anyway? I say. No, he says, you are right. Most people don't want to know. And what about Julia? I ask. (He had mentioned her when we were smoking.) I am her secret, he says. And I smile.

I think I was the one that broke up with her a few months later, which is why I hardly remember it. I just know we were together then, for a while, and then we weren't. I couldn't do it anymore. It wasn't the last time I'd think I could be cool, could handle our fucking, the other people, the mix of us that wasn't an us but was a habit, but like always it made me sad, and hungrier, and so I (think it was me who) stopped.

The anniversary morning comes with a chill and a touch of sun. Let's go to the house, I text Leroy, but it is mid-afternoon before we get there. He's convinced me to drink a Red Bull to perk up and the sick sweet is still stuck to my tongue. We park. Walk over. The grass has been cut recently. It's such an unremarkable place to live. Do you think they know? he asks. The air is cool and the sky ceiling of gray haze creates a nearness I wish I could escape from. Yellowed leaves plaster the pavement. It was news back then, I say, but who reads old news? Leroy nods. They interviewed dad on the lawn, I tell him: and what happened after you heard the crash? the newscaster asked, and dad told her we ran outside and she had said, all of you? and he had said, almost all of us. You can see me in the tape, I tell Leroy, there in the background, just standing off to the side, staring at the newscaster's soft-curl hair. (Dad didn't say that James had taken off, that we didn't know where he went. A week later when James got back, he had shaved his head and had the beginnings of a beard. Are you okay? my grandmother kept asking him. Should he not be? I asked. I don't know, I don't know, I was just asking—)

We hear a noise, like someone opening a door, and so Leroy and I turn and walk down the street, away from the house, across other lawns. I tell him I feel like it's happening now. Like right before the wreck. Our purposelessness has the same calm, the same readiness for interruption.

He knocks me with his elbow. Can you save them? he asks. Save them? I laugh. No, I say.

Besides, it didn't occur to me to want to.

Later we are overfull of hamburgers in the Columbia River Gorge, out of town because we can be, and I am debating whether I still want a milkshake. The menus have too many pictures and the food is barely seasoned. He reminds me we've got at least an hour's drive back into town. Evening has begun and I am restless. How far is Boise? I ask. What's in Boise? he says. I don't know, I say. That's the point.

We ride. Past the cascade locks the distance of the state line settles in and darkness crowds the road with treeless hills. I look for the moon, but it is new and hidden. Leroy takes the first leg and smokes quietly with his cigarette hanging between his fingers, deft and firm outside the lowered window. The high desert night is cold and Bjork sings into our small, mobile shelter. Leroy leans over and says Bjork is obviously an alien, and I say, do you think she is visiting just for a while, and he says she was probably born on a planet orbiting Betelgeuse. That's basically Iceland, I say, and he says basically, and we laugh and turn it up. Four hours in we pull off at an exit to pee. There is no sound but the whooshing of traffic. I pop a squat and Leroy faces the trees and smokes another cig while he waters the tall grass.

How long do you think you'll stay here? he asks, and I say, I don't know. It seems like such a dead-end place, he says and shakes off. Just an oil slick of white dreamers on top of a deep lake of white supremacy, he says. We're white, I say, and he says, yes, it makes it easier, doesn't it? And I say I have always wanted to go east, and I stand to zip, and he says the east is full of cynics, but it is good for cutting teeth. Do you miss Pennsylvania? I ask, as we trade off and I take the wheel. I miss the winter, he says, and the hardness of everyone. I wouldn't expect that to be missed, I say. All these kumbayahyah liberals don't actually know how to tolerate difference, he says, gesturing back at Portland. They're just comfort whores passing off their sameness as progressivism. I'd rather be around a bunch of redneck anarchos, fighting with their Black neighbors against the police than this bunch of craft beer stand-for-nothings. Support Obama, my ass.

I'd never heard anyone say anything so mean about Portland, but what he says feels true, and so I say I agree.

We drive. Time dilates. I get sleepy, must've slept, because soon we are there. Boise comes with the sunrise and it is a plain brick town, western, with opportunity in its best corners and rancid bigots in its worst. I'm hungry and my spit is thick. We do not linger. I buy us breakfast sandwiches and then we turn around and drive back to Portland, taking shifts to nap. The road is too long. Boise was a mistake, but I don't mind it so much, because we had each other on the road. Past The Dalles the green really kicks in, but I can't remember if I ever thought it was beautiful. When I am awake and still a passenger, I watch the water for sturgeon or some other great creature, but I see only the gold glistening waves. Leroy is tired and Portland is still three hours away. When we switch off he says he doesn't know what he wants from a home yet. Me either, I say, and we do not stop until we are back. Five months after our overnight to Idaho, he leaves first and suddenly. He sells everything and buys a one-way ticket to New York, says it is temporary. He has no plan, and the gumption of it tricks me into trusting I could too. I do not see him for over a year, but the idea of it gets into me, and the distance across the states seems smaller. I save. My mom cries when I tell her. I decide not to talk about it again. Besides, I don't owe her my life.

3

Time has passed—too much. It's March in Brooklyn and I'm over the snow seven weeks ago. Leroy's living in Asheville now and we love each other across the distance in phone calls and emails and text messages. He only lasted a year in NYC. Fuck, I get it. I get up. Saturday means laundry and avoiding people I know in the neighborhood. Tomorrow I'll get lonely and text them to meet me at Crown. I've been pulling executive assistant duty in some richo's office on the Upper East Side, riding the 4 past Grand Central with all the Dominican and Mexican domestic workers and watching the days go by like so many to-dos. But Saturday is mine. I drop in the first load and head back to my room. Take a break from scrolling through facebook to look at porn. I start out with softcore pics but then open a few tabs for hardcore videos. I come hard and fast watching a girl lick her lips too slow and thinking about what's-his-name I hooked up with on Wednesday. Chris? White and slick like a piece of pressure-washed concrete. I usually like them hairier if I'm swinging that way, but he was enough for the night. Not Chris—Aaron.

Was it two(?) years previous that I moved to the city on a plane with my books boxed up on a plastic-wrapped pallet riding on Amtrak to NJ—sold everything else? Picked it all up in a rental car and brought it to Brooklyn. The first four months were just me and an air mattress with Lean Cuisines, a bottle of Sriracha and too much trash. Books everywhere. It was a healthy dose of poverty tourism, but it only lasted ten months before I bought my first Ikea bookshelf and coffee table and then saved up for something midcentury from one of the secondhand stores. It's fucked up but I feel closer to my cowhide rug than most people in the city some days. Not sure if that says more about me or the quality of who I meet. Doesn't matter. This is what I'm living in and with, and for now I'm not looking for a way out. I want to see how this goes.

Home is what it is. Mom's with the worst fucker she's met in a decade. I used to hate her for never having a new idea, but now that her mistakes are three thousand miles away, it's easier to recognize her sadness for the resignation it is. She gave up on whatever she once hoped her life could be before I was even born. I guess after you do that, one big mistake or ten thousand small ones are all the same. And dad's got a new family, at least a better wife with kids on the way—why would he bother with the complications of my unhappiness?

The goal for these forty-eight hours is to forget that the other assistant in my office is an orange-skinned white girl from Florida with self-assured opinions and snuggie-blanket ignorance. Too easy to shrink myself into equivalencies. I get restless at the thought of our lives running parallel. I shift the load to the dryer and think maybe it's okay to be a bad neighbor when you need to, and then abandon everything, hit the subway, and head to Rudy's on the west side. It's a good place to remember other nights, drunk and laughing in the red duct-tape-covered booths. I was in love with M, then, and I was squished between him and Lawrence and Lawrence kept running his hand up my thigh under the table even though it was M who I was kissing. It had been three days since I'd been home and my hair smelled like the mint shampoo M loved. I knew when we got back to his apartment we would drink grapefruit juice and gin and I would strip and beg him to fuck me with our sweating skin sliding on each other on his couch. M looked younger than his years, with his shaved face and tousled hair. I wasn't ready to build more than this hour, then the next, together, but it didn't matter. He accepted me as I was, in my worst mess and broken self-doubt, even on late nights when I would pilgrimage to his bed, and the view from his window as I rode him: a single tree spreading for heaven in a courtyard of concrete beyond the window.

I sit at the corner of the bar and order a beer. When it comes, I hunch over it like a prisoner over his midday meal. At this moment I do not know that I will see Lex coming out of a gallery on W Broad in SoHo three months later and I do not know that the sun will hit the doorjamb above her like the goddamn finger of god and I do not know I will forget heartache and concrete courtyards and that I ever made a mistake once, twice, a thousand times. The time since I left Portland will collapse like an arrow pointing directly to that moment, a chance to pick up where I lost my best hope to pride, and I will say Lex? and I will be new, to her and to me. Right now though, I am full of worry and misunderstanding, wishing a life's meaning could be bought like a candle that says Serenity, burning slowly of camellias in a dirty bathroom. I am hard on myself because I am accustomed to internalizing my mother's casual judgment. Even when she is not around, I know the ways that she has given up believing I will make her proud. Too much debt, not enough children, career success, anything. It is easier to blame me for all the ways my story does not mimic the children of the other people she knows than admit she and I never understood each other to begin with. When will you settle down? she asks. When will you stop drinking? I never say. I finger the coaster under my beer. I scratch my nails on my thighs under the bar and try to forget.

Later I'm passed out on the couch when one of my housemates comes in with his best friend and too many groceries for two people to carry with four arms. They plonk the full plastic bags on the floor of the kitchen and the sound startles me up from the blanket-covered couch where I must've crashed when I got home. The time? Time . . . time . . . the light is new afternoon and the children laughing outside mean Sunday. Oh shit, my laundry. I trudge in my socks and wince with the light and joy of Charles' and his buddy's conversation. Brunch is on the make. A hot shower washes off the beer of the day before and I throw on a pair of dirty jeans, sneaks, a sweater, scarf, and coat before going back to the mat, sniffing my clothes, deciding I can wing it, and then drying them again. Doesn't take long before that's all taken care of and I'm careening again into the world.

It's me vs. New York except New York already won. I text Cecilia. She's feeling guilty for drunk dialing her ex at 2 a.m. the night before. We decide to head to the MET and get lost snaking through the galleries. By the time I pop out of the subway at 86th Street she's just texted me she can't make it—too hung over, and I don't know what I was expecting anyway. I wander over to Museum Mile alone. The wives of the men that my boss calls can be seen walking the streets with their dogs and their children. Dior, Gucci, YSL. It's like an issue of *Vanity Fair* exploded in the traffic.

At the museum I expect better, but better requires patient searching. I'm not the kind of good aesthete that loves what is beautiful because it is on display in the right place with the right commentary; I'm more the hissing cockroach, ready for tight quarters. I click-clack through the armor room, move on to other exhibitions, lean and judge, find one or two pieces that impress me, and then bail for a walk south. I hit Midtown before sundown and keep going, as though the stop and go sliding of taxis between buildings have a contagious truth, something about perpetual motion, about any given person's relationship to the clock. We're in this together and it's getting cooler with nightfall. I quicken my pace. Anonymous men and women stream by and I believe I give an impression of purpose even as my mind drifts back to that feeling of high school, of frantic impatience to be an adult, to be able to steer my own life. Was it because of that first post-college job that I realized the kind of autonomy and freedom available to me would always be contingent on some desk ball and chain? Or was it later? I couldn't place it. It didn't matter. There wasn't a way to return to that new penny hope. The life-preserving option was this contemplative circle-jerking amongst the squeaky clean.

She's in bed, asleep, beside me, and I'm watching the sunlight make a line on the wall across from us, vertical and sharp like a furnace-hot sword. This morning I remember like a flash-fast montage of moments that I have held onto, that for so long I carried with me, folded in my pocket for those hours of dread and dead, when I would need to remind myself that surprises always come. She came, we came, it came about like this: after the first run-in, the surprise, the nervous smile, she called me (she called me!) this time and we went to Branded and ate chicken fingers and drank whiskey-bacon milkshakes and I laughed too loud and it didn't matter. She told me about her cousin drowning the year before, how she had had to fly back to the city and how she'd touched her cousin's small, dead fingers—everyone looks so small when they're gone—and how after that she couldn't hang around Portland, couldn't hang on a thread so far away. She wanted the freedom that New York was so good at pretending to offer, and so she had moved back, gotten a day job, and settled in. She said the show in Soho was only a couple pieces—but I'm proud of them, she said—and we were older and less haunted by what we thought it meant to be grown, and more sure of what life we were building. I told her about the stories and poems I'd published, a few here and there, how I felt like I needed to live a little more before I had anything real to say, and she laughed, and said of course I would say that.

It continued, and by continued, I mean we checked in with each other every couple weeks, then every few days. I invited her to Charles' first house show and Cecilia's dj set in Bushwick. We got drunk in front of M during his late shift on the Upper West Side and I glanced at him now and then and he would smile at me and I would smile at him, the way you smile when you'll always love someone no matter who they are, who they become, no matter what you had to do to be free to be best version of yourselves. She wore the city slipped on and rough from the first years knocking around in the LES when it was still a place to be, now seams ripped, now disappointed but not given up, as she saw the richos move in where she'd dreamed on childhood evenings of other somewheres. The sun was brighter because I was drunk with her. My old clothes were new because they reminded me of where she had been. I called mom and she said I just want you to be happy, I'm so glad that you're happy. We don't say we're together; we aren't ever apart. We work, we wrestle around, we drift into summer on the heat of early evenings spent by the water, laughing at garbage, the city small before our lust.

It was early enough that I was in that sun flare of forgetfulness. I forgot that the Floridation blonde had been driving me nuts and I forgot that being tired can be a bad thing and I forgot how old I might have become because none of it mattered, really. I was in fucking love and full of wind and strong strides; I felt large and complete and like my life belonged to me. Everest was littered with dead bodies, but my mountain top was pristine and near and always with me.

We were irresponsible with money and we were serious about leisure. One night in the intoxication of her laugh I asked her to the roof of my building and we sat on a blanket and drank mismixed mojitos as the sun went down and the city faded into black-blue sparkle. The neighbors fought and I thought of the highs and lows of this cyclone, this us, and knew I would cry someday and knew that was okay because right now was still ours, and full of the possibility of her, right here, right near. In the morning I woke with reluctance, but there was a joy behind my eyes as I wand-stroked my lashes with mascara. She would see those eyes. I would see her with those eyes. It was ridiculous. I was ridiculous. I had never known how purely love could infuse the background of an unremarkable life with glory.

She was doing well, as though the spark of us was a lucky charm and she was safe to jump from bridges and cliffs without fear of falling. She took more chances with form, and her paintings melted into contour fury and strident neon. I was jealous of the paint, without reason, and wished that I could drop into her hand and make something as beautiful as the abstract fever dreams of her worst days. It is embarrassing to remember then. It seems so foolish to obsess over one person with such fervor. In other times I have eaten the same melted grilled cheese for dinner every night, and it never occurred to me that the pattern was the thing until the pattern broke. Our togetherness had the same eternal quality as it happened, as though we had always been and always would. She was what I knew and would know. Next week would come and we would talk and fuck like the week before. That is the mystery of feeling: it's ability to erase the past and future as though they were merely suggestions, small whispers of someone else's life in your ear.

When mom called from the side of the road in Portland, too drunk to tell me more than "I was drivin" and "cops now" Lex looked at me and gave me permission to hate. I hung up the phone. I didn't speak to my mother for a year. In that silence I built a church. My breath was my liturgy. Lex and I talked about moving in together, and I started looking for something cheap in Astoria—as it was, Greek and Egyptian and full of eurotrashy dinner spots with bright lighting and too-good wine for the price. My temp daygrind turned into a full-time spot and I manned the desk and made small talk and texted Lex in-between expense reports.

On the weekend, we sipped hotel bottles of liquor along the East River, trespassing behind warehouses with sloppy kisses. We were like a goddamn American Apparel ad without the pedophilic gaze, just pure panysian youth, grotesque and beautiful and deeply in debt. My credit score held steady at 650 something anyway, which is good enough to seem good to some brokers, and we rented a one bedroom off 37th Street and Broadway in Queens, close to four train lines but quiet enough that we could leave the window open in the spring.

She hangs her two favorite paintings in the bedroom and I see her as she is, before she puts on her costume for the gallery assistant gig that keeps the lights on. She gets good at kissing the dollar-boosted asses of the blessed, who buy culture from a catalogue in a concrete room they would have scoffed at ten years before. I get suspicious of her smiles; I hate that I am so easily afraid of what they contain. We have drunken brunch each Saturday, then fuck, then nap, then venture into the midnight air to suss up different fun in booths and bar seats, secreted in the dark of warm corners and vodka-soaked floors. She knows the bouncers. She knows so-and-so who's having a party in BedStuy. She knows how to get a spot on the roof of the Jimmy without paying for drinks. People meet me like I'm lucky. Men shake my hand like what moxie. It's always the quiet ones, she says, and winks at me through whirling murmurs.

I see the texts when she leaves her phone behind on a hungover morning in October, sixteen months in. Vibrate, alert, and the screen lights up with heartache. She comes home all smiles and kisses my neck while I stir onions on the stove, staring at the swirling pieces as they brown. You know people are the only mammals that can eat onions, she says, nibbling my ear. Maybe because we are just as rotten inside, I say. What the fuck is up with you? she says, and I turn off the stove. I haven't practiced this. I'm not good at practicing anything. It comes out or it doesn't. It comes out. She doesn't deny it. I ask who she is. She says a friend from the gallery. A friend? I ask.

She's older. She's a patron. It's fucked every way I look at it. I feel like a joke. She starts crying. Sits at the table. I know better, she says. I know better. Do you think we pick up? I said. Do you think this is something we can survive? I say. I hate myself. I don't want to survive this. I'm dead and then I am screaming, GET THE FUCK OUT. She picks up the bag she had dropped by the door, grabs her phone off the kitchen counter and leaves.

Silence. I return to the stove and stir the onions. The absence of her is like the air after lightning. I wait for thunder, but there is only ordinary noise. Add ground beef. Stir to brown. Tomato sauce, salt, pepper, Italian seasoning, red pepper flakes. Boil the water. Drain the pasta. Mix and plate. Pour a glass of too-long-open sauvignon. Night happens, then waking, a commute, work, repeat. Cecilia calls me and leaves a message. Same-same for two weeks. One Friday I come home and Cecilia is waiting for me in front of my building and asking me if I'm okay.

No, I am not okay. My rent is twice as expensive. My heart is fucked. Her stuff is still here. Too much of it. I am living in a museum of my old happiness. We go upstairs. Cecilia listens, quietly throws away candy wrappers and empty microwave dinner boxes and napkins and used ziploc bags with leftover crumbs and cheese powder, from the kitchen. She wets a sponge. She nods as she wipes down the counter. Bro, you can't live like this, she says. She is tender. I know better, I say. I know better. We finish the kitchen and move to the bedroom. In the corner she piles Lex's folded tshirts, her jeans. I add Lex's rusted nail sculpture from the dresser, a few of her art books I wish I could keep out of revenge (but know I'd just cry into), her underwear, everything I can find. It's an ugly pile, falling over on itself and unsorted like trash. Why did we move in together again? Why?

I remember when Gere came to visit, Lex picked at her french fries, and he was wearing civilian clothes for easier blending amongst the plebs. He had plugs in his ears. I didn't ask. Even though the things he did were always because of a new way he had found to assert his belonging in this or that subculture, he never failed to use some *sadhana* to explain them. I have read that the human brain is a master at rationalization, and I will admit that in this practice, my brother has always been a fucking yogi. What did I know, even, about her? I believed we were a unit, or at least had become one, and the presence of any of my family members seemed to affirm that.

The way I remember it, it was good to see him with her there, because I did not feel crazy that I thought him self-involved, that I found his stories pedantic, his compliments backhanded. She squeezed my leg under the table when he launched into an explanation of why I just needed to align my chakras, as though my frustration and anxiety had a simple solution I was too dense to acknowledge. I tried to keep it light. How is your visit going? Where are you headed next? And she would mention the new exhibit of East Indian antiquities at the MET. He hugged me and whispered something in my ear that must have been sanskrit—a blessing maybe—but felt like a curse, like a symbol of everything ineffable in the gap between us. She fucked me in the taxi home, her hand slipped into my pants as I looked out the window, pretending we were a family. There was no rationalization in me when it came to her, just action and lust and a hunger to have it continue, unending and near.

Cecilia tells me it would be good to have her things gone and I believe her because I could feel myself touching Lex's shirts like precious artifacts, drifting into the spun romance of a past that never existed. Cecilia agrees I should text Lex to pick up everything or maybe just deliver it all to her, because maybe it's better to have it gone. Maybe she shouldn't come here? Cecilia is good at using maybe like a pillow, and I say yeah, and I text Lex after we eat dinner. The next morning, after Cecilia stays over, holding me as I cry myself to sleep, we get up and put all of Lex's stuff in bags and spend an hour on the subway so we can meet Lex at some rando's apartment on 14th Street in Manhattan.

She opens the door and her jaw is as sharp and beautiful as the first time I kissed it. She is wearing a loose tank dress; I haven't seen her in a dress since my dad's wedding. Here, I say. Yeah, she says. We hand over the bags one at a time and she sets them down past the threshold where I am not allowed. Thanks for bringing everything by, she says. And I say no problem, and nod, and we are gone.

I hope for disaster as we leave, something bigger than us that could dwarf what drama we have created for ourselves in our heartache. I want to focus on a different pain. Cecilia offers to buy me lunch, which turns into a drunk afternoon and a late-night purchase: plane tickets to Asheville for the next weekend, courtesy of my credit card. I spend the next week in the past, running through flashes of her laughing, her eyes watching me from across the room, and the emptiness of the bed, bereft of our bodies. And then I am gone.

Leroy offers me a cigarette as soon as we exit the airport. We stand in the cool mountain air and he doesn't ask me anything. A lot of turbulence, I say, in between drags, and he says he's glad I made it, and smiles. At his place, we whine away the hours with stories of our jobs between puffs of pot and frequent snacking. The afternoon light is golden and his couch smells like my grandmother's chair, before she died, when I was young and reading Nancy Drews in her room while she picked her way through *Reader's Digest* on the bed. I believed in the eternality of afternoons and the shortness of life, then. But my religion has changed. Every moment with Leroy is too quick, too soon before I have to return to

Brooklyn, and these days, no matter where I go, I carry with me the complacent weariness of adulthood.

He shows me a book he stole from the library with hand-scrawled notes written in the margins by a long-dead woman. She wrote them as she voyaged from Miami to New York. *The weather has turned gloomy,* she says, *and I am still too heartsick to fight it. 1909.* What other wilds, I wonder, might I have had in some past era? I always think I would have ended up a suffragette or prostitute back then, I say. Or both, he says. Sex work gets a bad rap, I say—what the hell else were you supposed to do if you didn't want to get married? Become a teacher? A nun? And if you didn't like kids or didn't believe in god? And if you wanted economic power? I rant and rant. It's still good money, he says. I've thought about it, I say. The quickest way to move capital from the surreally wealthy to the rest of us. I'd probably start with foot parties.

He laughs. Your feet are pretty cute, he says. We drink white wine with ice cubes tinkling against the glass. He beckons me to the porch and we stare into the dark of the neighbor's back yard, blankets wrapped around our shoulders. I am as in love with him as I have always been; it is the best relationship of my life. When he finally asks me what happened, recent events spill from my mouth.

In response, he offers to read my tarot, to tell me what the future will be. I avoid the chance.

The cards sit stacked between us as he finishes his glass of wine. She never saw you clearly, he says, and leaves me with those words, just words, and he is right (I think?). She is so quickly a ghost to me, all loss and a shape that I loved. I hate that I do not know better, that I cannot conjure up more than some vague throbbing—and then I wonder if any relationships are not this internal fantasy, so quickly blurred? What do I know—she is gone.

He spoons me in his bed that night, warm and small. I was seeing this guy, he says. Did you meet him online, I ask. Yeah. I'm not really into the scene here anyway. It's easier that way. He was married, he says, and I don't mind that so much—honestly, I don't think I'm even looking for a partner anymore, he says. I think I've always been looking for a surprise, but surprises are hard to find. Anyway, I met him at his house when his wife was out of town, quick blowjobs, you know, nothing special—and the place was fucking filthy, and while I'm peeing in the bathroom I hear this car drive up and it's his boyfriend fucking pissed. I'm like, the fuck, you have a boyfriend AND a wife? I'm out. He's like, I'm poly, we have an understanding, but this dude in the yard, you can tell by his voice that the only understanding he has is that some strange dude's pickup is blocking his boyfriend's driveway. The fuck you doing, Chuck? he keeps yelling. Leroy breaks down laughing and I'm laughing. How'd you get out, I say? I walked out and saluted him, he says. I'm on my back and he's on his back and we're clutching our bellies because we can hardly breathe. You fucking saluted him? I say. Yes, he screams, his voice soaring. And then I got in my truck, did a U-ey and got the fuck out. Almost hit a turkey on the way down the road, I was going so fast. That's some redneck shit, I say. Turkey trouble, he says, and we both lose it again. I get up because I'm gonna pee myself and I run to the bathroom, slipping my pants off and yelling at him to shut the fuck up, I'm dying.

We settle after this, in the quiet echo of what was our laughter, and with my eyes closed, I try to clock the feel of the bed, the difference in the shape of him and the shape of her, the memory of the single I slept in when James was still James and mom and dad were still pretending, and then I remember college, and the small bed of my room and the heaviness of the blankets, and my certain dread that I did not belong there, but feeling just as certain that it was the best place to be, because I did not know where else to go. He wakes me up with coffee; he has done this before. I know I am more palatable after two cups, more open to the noise of whatever humans I find myself near, even if they are beloved. Let's go to the tracks, he says, and I know that he means somewhere particular and so I get dressed and we take cheese and crackers and slim jims and water in a pack and I've got a bandana around my neck just in case.

It's gray like Portland and Leroy walks ahead of me, with his knobby, sanded staff clunking against the rail ties. He wears loose jeans and a sleek hoodie. I'm as comfortable as I ever get since I lost the smooth lines of my string-bean years. More curves in the woods, I am, and so we walk side by side and then front by back on the railroad in a valley by a river that has cut through the mountains and made passage from the ordinary to the other. We pass rusted wrecks of agricultural equipment stashed in Cold War dugouts lined in cinder blocks and littered with faded porn magazines. We meander to the water and back again to the rails, the right-of-way our line of regression, with its meaning and predictions still to come in the analysis.

I knew without knowing that day that Lex and I were not done with each other, but I had no shape for us, and so it was clear we were done for a long while. I threw myself into present-living; the wind was cold and my hair was damp and I wanted to be warm and feel powerful and so we built a fire by the water, amidst cairns of stacked rocks. Leroy waved a makeshift torch at the four corners, banishing whatever outside haunts might have followed us and all the heartache I still harbored. If it had been warmer I would have stripped my clothes away and drifted in the river, like I had in the waters of other afternoons in Oregon, in other woods, where we once walked to find a new way home.

It was always us, I say.

He pokes at the fire and throws in dried grass from the embankment. We let an hour pass. Then we return to the rails. I carry a penny that's been smashed smooth and lost by some other train watcher. As we wind back to his truck he stops and lays his ear on the rail. It's coming, he says, and I am with him, and we turn and wait for the thundering passage of the locomotive.

4

She came through the door so happy and I've never hated her more. She, my mother, she, in jeans, in a tshirt, gray now with a golden oldie drunk on her arm: Brenda's husband, his real name something super white like Blake or Brent, who cares. I didn't want to care. It was only the second time I'd seen him in person, but he was as repugnant in his patterned tent shirts and too-tight shorts as the first time I'd clocked his leering at her in the public pool.

I looked at Lex, wanted to tell her I hated this with my eyes, but I know I pleaded with her instead, my eyebrows betraying me. This was back when we were still together—visiting Portland from Astoria, back before I cut mom out of my life and Lex cut me out of hers. Or I cut her out of mine? It depends on what you consider a cut, or what counts as an absence. Lex spoke, said welcome home, because it was mom's apartment anyway, and then she joined them in the kitchen, pouring water for everyone. I stayed on the couch, collecting my awe at Lex's composure, and then fixed my face. My fake smile was good and reasonable, I reasoned, because my cheeks hurt from the attempt. They tumbled into the living room and mom said, why don't you girls go for a walk, and I didn't need a second hint. We hit the sidewalk and headed for Westmoreland, where the drunks were at least classy enough to keep it hidden behind pruned hedges, closed doors, and dark curtains. Money has always been the best dress for addiction.

We ambled slowly, the evening sky like a cavern ceiling, and us, in the dark, shrouded by our separateness in the waning day. I wanted to make Lex know my loneliness, how deep and singular my hatred for my mother was, her insecurity, her desire to be saved, her victimhood, her messy life, but I did not know how to share that feeling. The crumble of what childhood respect I had kept for my mother had been crushed by her repeated falsities and sarcasm, and it was a loss of love that I still mourned like the acute and personal death of an imaginary friend. You are always so sharp when it comes to your mom, said Lex as we passed a house with the drapes slightly open, giving a peek of the golden light and orange couch within. Kind of like you with your dad, I said. Her faced flashed a moment of recognition, as though the record had skipped and the skip itself was the song I wanted to hear.

I was being mean. I wanted her vulnerability. It was not enough that she loved me. My heart craved the view no others were allowed. I need to know you are not stronger than me, I could not say, and so I said to her, why didn't you kill him?

She laughed. I still could, she said. He deserves it, I say. If every man who'd fucked a girl that didn't want it was killed, there wouldn't be many men left, she said. Sure, but what about the fathers who did? I asked. I don't know that it makes that much difference, she said. Maybe not, I said, and my selfish want for that broken nugget of her joy was lost to my own sadness again. There was more she would never tell, I knew, and we would have to love around the unspoken traumas that made us each the people we were, walking now in the dark, without aim, to avoid the drunken moans of my mom.

And goddamn it, Lex was easy to love. In the soft light of the street lamps and the wet evening air, she ran ahead of me and yelled, let's go, and so we ran because we could, at breakneck speed down the tree-lined avenue until we were in front of the college, and then we turned further west, and she was making fun of me as I awkwardly scaled the fence of the public golf course after her. We ran across the damp greens and my hair tossed with my uneven gait and she was ahead, and then over the hill and then recessed where I would follow. Take off your shoes, she said, and we dug our toes into the cool sand of the traps and she dropped to the ground and cupped fistfuls of it in her hands, shaping it into mounds and more mounds until we had built castles in the moonlight.

I don't want to go back, I said, as I traced windows into the sand wall beside me. She was quiet. What I could read of her body, leaning slant and lovely along a dip of deep sand, was a fierce attention towards what might come next. I felt farthest from her when I most loved her. I want to see where you grew up, she said, and I was surprised, but I said okay, and so we went in the morning.

We stood where I used to stand with Leroy on our returns and stared at the now-teal front door as though any minute the girl inside me would emerge. The house was still a plain ranch with seventies cedar siding. The grass, spotty. The neighbors were still there, at least some of them, and the ones that had died or moved on had been replaced by young families whose plastic tyke tricycles and play kitchens now littered their yards. Can you imagine dying here? I said. No, she said, it's why I moved back to New York. Yes, I thought. And it's why I left as soon as I could.

There's nothing left for you here, said Lex. No, I said. I knew it, but I wanted a better close. The clouds surrounded us, as if we had risen or they had fallen—I could not tell which. It was colder. We went back to mom's apartment and didn't speak much on the drive. Took a nap on the blow-up mattress at the foot of her bed. The room smelled like laundry detergent and wet plaster.

Lex snored and I fell asleep watching the curtains, so still and unmoved. We left before sunrise.

I hated Portland as much as (or because of?) my constant urge to return to the scene of my origins. It made no sense to keep coming back. While I justified every return as a check-in to make sure mom was, at least, functional, going back felt instead like a test of who I had become. That: a woman with debt, with love (now and then), an unremarkable job. Yes, I had been published a few times—that part of the early dream had been realized. Lex always said I should give myself more credit. I said, tell that to the landlord. Say it to me again.

On the flight home I asked her why we never visited with her childhood friends in the city and she said she didn't like holding on to people—it made her feel crowded, like she was drowning in old possibilities. Onward, onward, relentlessly. I had never met someone so sure, so future-minded and unburdened. She had walked onto the plane like she had designed it, had walked down the aisle like it was her red carpet. She never acknowledged the stares of lesser people so unused to a woman so unabashedly butch. Her head shaved, jeans low. Her tank tight across her bound breasts—a habit she dipped in and out of depending on what presentation suited her—and her hoodie loose, hanging almost like a cape around her solid figure. I could not look at her without measuring my breath. That others could be repulsed by her singular and statuesque devil-may-care saunter infuriated me. I grew to trust public spaces as far as they could admit her. I was a knight defending her queen. I had forgotten how to smile.

We clung to New York like it could give us purpose, make our lives bigger and more significant by proxy. Or maybe we just wanted an otherwhere with fewer ghosts and more chances to rise and fail. That fall was breezy and brisk with throngs of hurried and determined faces enlivened by the crisp air and swirling leaves. We huddled under the covers together, cursing the landlord for waiting until the last possible minute to finally turn on the radiator. We texted each other when we were headed home. So many late-night movies: she loved Bollywood, I didn't, but it didn't matter. I didn't know she would be gone in a year. I didn't know what future hurt would magnify those easy evenings.

Should I have? The Christmas after she is gone I stay up late watching SVU to drown out the looping rationalizations and self-blame, thinking I should have known she was fucking someone else. I didn't know if she loved that woman, and I never asked. In the midst of my loneliness I become angry even at myself for my skin-crawling rage. I have never believed fidelity should be the only measure of a relationship's functioning or even the deal-breaker when it isn't offered. But that was before I'd understood obsession, or whatever's the best word for this heart-sick, clinging intoxication. I text mom merry something. Same thing to dad. I show up an hour early to work every day, knocking out projects that I'd put off before because of a blasé dgaf attitude.

Cecilia decides we should tour the city with our stomachs. One week we eat soup dumplings in Queens, another week we're laugh-crying our way through spicy doubles at one of the last surviving Trinidadian places on Nostrand Ave. Then it's on to Italian in Tribeca and pierogis in Greenpoint. After she finds a Nepali place, I suggest this Uzbek-Russian spot on Coney Island Avenue and we sit for hours, eating plov and drinking tea with jam. She says her mother used to tell her that you must feed your stomach to heal your heart, and I tell her I believe that, and I do not tell her that I wish my mother was dead.

When, in late January, I hear through the grapevine that Lex has taken a new job at a bigger gallery and one of her paintings is supposed to appear in a group show in London, I eat lamb and rice from the halal cart by my office every day for a week. Cecilia says I should go to the Cubby, that it would help if I, ya know, spent time with my friends, that Yvonne will be there and Claire and Trish and what the fuck am I doing on Friday anyway. I roll out like I'm told, and I wear my best jeans because I want to feel sexy around these other women, so good at living their own lives on their own terms. I spot Trish first, her dark locs in a knot on her head and sunglasses still on her face because she doesn't give a fuck. She's whispering to a blonde femme by the restroom, and I smile at her when I pass. Claire's at the bar, nursing a gin and tonic, and I sit down. She works at a skate shop in SoHo where she mixes youtube videos on the spot sort of how Cecilia mixes records in Bushwick these days, but the technology is three laptops and two button boards she codes herself. She's got blue jewels and a yellow plastic pick in her afro. I sit next to her and she says, hey stranger. Halfway through my first beer, Yvonne comes in and the room parts. I hear at least one audible gasp. She's Chinese and Danish, at least six feet tall and more like a goddess than a person. I don't think I've ever heard a single man believe her when she says she's gay—in my experience they think lesbians only like each other because they can't get a man. It doesn't occur to them that the same women they can't get enough of might not be able to get enough of each other. She belts at the bartender in a good growl, whiskey with a Bud chaser, and Cecilia slaps her ass (when did she come in?), then leans over me: told you this would be good for you. We all get shitfaced and stumble through the Village to Henrietta's then over to the park on the Westside, where Trish dares me to do a cartwheel on the concrete. I land it but crumple down laughing, and Claire gives me a hand up but trips and joins me on the ground.

Come on you guys, the sky! she screams. And then we're all lying in a drunken circle, staring at what stars are bright enough to show through the dark light haze.

I fucking love this city, says Cecilia. I don't, says Claire. Smells like piss and maggots. WTF do maggots smell like, asks Yvonne and laughs. Like your ass, I say, and we're all laughing and then Cecilia's like, shut up you know Yvonne's ass smells like Chanel No. 5, and I say what sweet cunt is lucky enough to know that? And Claire says, like you haven't heard. And I'm like, what? And she's like, Lex never told you? And I'm like fuckkkkkkk and suddenly sober and running awayyyyyy.

Slap crack slap—the hard street rhythms carry me to the first crowded corner where I hail a cab I can't afford and tell the driver to take me back to Brooklyn. I'm halfway up the stoop before I realize I don't live here anymore. I sit and cry into my scarf, bent in half over my knees. Charles shows up an hour later. It's two in the morning when he taps on my shoulder. V? Yeah, I say. Come in, he says. I follow his swishing skirt up to my old door, his current door, and everything smells different—like incense and roasted chicken. Go sit on the couch, babe, he says, and changes into a caftan before bringing me some tea. I heard about the breakup, he says. I'm sorry, I say, I was drunk and forgot I didn't live here anymore. He waves my words away. How's the label going? I ask. Sporadically, he says. The warehouse is doing an open house next month, if you wanna come. Yes, I say. I don't know how to get away from her, I say. She's not here, he says, and goes to get me a blanket.

She's not here, I say, I say, I say, I say.

5

My dress was itchy at my grandmother's funeral. It was a brown dress, I remember, some polyester blend with a wide collar—too old for me, really—but it hung on my newly pubescent frame better than my usual uniform of cutoff shorts and buttonups that didn't quite fit over my new breasts.

The sky spat at us gathered graveside. She was so small in the coffin and the coffin so large. A preacher spoke—one I had seen before—and dad cried. Gere said it was too much trouble to travel back. Mom kept her arm threaded through dad's elbow, like if she let go she might lose him. And he nodded at everyone who said they were so sorry, so sorry for his loss. What could he say? The woman who gave him life was painted with grease makeup and buried in the ground.

It was the first time I had really known grief. Before then, I had believed grief had a shape with borders and limits and an end. But after gran died, I knew it was a feeling that could become a hum and then a volcano and sometimes an ocean. Bells rang at a church near the cemetery, and I imagined the worshippers filing onto the lawn with smiles and children screaming, so relieved to speak again after the service. Staring at my grandmother's coffin, my own mind drifted towards what nebulous ideas I held about divinity, and then unbeing, before my thoughts became tears full of sadness and fatigue and fear.

After a year, then two, then more, that feeling faded like a tapestry in a sunlit room. And then in unexpected moments, it would insist on itself again. Breakups and divorces, disappointments and failures, all summoned the old hurt, and I began to wonder if every heartache wasn't just practice for the eternal separation between the living and the dead. As with any loss, it is not the dead who suffer, but the steady flaming fools left behind.

In my dream the baba yaga cackled in the grove, naked and wrinkled, with her gray spindly pubic hair laughing with her. She beckoned me into the chicken-footed house and served me tea made of water from stones. I drank and saw Lex, sad and quiet, sitting at our old kitchen table and staring out the window. Her hair had grown in and she was ready for another buzz. The wrinkles in her shirt made her look dirtier than she was. Of all the people I have watched, she never had an empty look; her eyes were full of plans, at once terrifying and delicious. But her back was to me, and I busied myself around her, dressing hurriedly for work, barking questions about the location of my keys, putting in my earrings, brushing my hair, before breathing relief to be away from her, on my way to the raised subway and far from the very intensity that compelled me to her to begin with. A premonition. The alarm went off and my vision went black. How dead I lived in my grief.

With Lex gone, I considered counseling, but my past experience with it had soured me against that version of self-care. After the head in the grass and my deepening childhood silence, I had been sent to someone by the adults, they who I think were my parents, my teachers, and the stranger-professionals who had come to clean up the mess of bodies and metal in our yard. My counselor was a stout woman who liked to eat crackers during our sessions. Her name was Ms. Stanos. I have always hated crumbs on tables and I hated them on her breasts the same, distracted as I was by her crunching. Let us break bread together, she would say, and hand me a cracker very formally, which I would nibble on and then set aside, thinking, in my childhood logic: this isn't even bread. Tell me what happened, she would say. And I would wait until I could tell she would feel especially satisfied by my speaking and then I would run the tape again, rewinding and replaying, waiting for her to seize on something she found significant.

In retrospect I doubt she was even a psychoanalyst. As an adult I've learned how easy it is for someone to call themselves a counselor, while the certifications and training for therapists is more stringent. Counselor-anybody can be a numbskull with a real "heart for people." Regardless, I got the message quickly—that I was supposed to be scarred. I began to provide an excellent show of dramatic trauma. James stopped calling me Blank and started calling me Locktite, a shift I preferred, as it acknowledged, at least, that my silence was not (had never been) empty.

What I learned in those sessions, besides the ability to stand unbent beneath the pitying gaze of misunderstanding adults, I could not tell you. I did not know how to be seen and I did not want to see. Sex, as an adult, was often a similar navigation of connection, ever elusive. Leroy told me one afternoon as we watched the clouds pass during a perfect Oregon August that he didn't think people ever really encountered each other, but met, instead, each other's avatars—redrawn and revised, daily. I hated this idea because it presupposed defeat, as though true seeing was never really possible. Do we get closer to seeing when it is two people of the same gender? I asked, and he said that's the pretty lie we like to tell ourselves, isn't it? No, he said, it is always only people—different people—looking at each other, looking for themselves.

I fell for Sarah in middle school back when our coach called her HeartAttack because he swore she was gonna give him one the way she teased our opponents with her deft ball maneuvers and drives. She had giant posters of Mia Hamm on her wall and knew more trick shots than any of the rest of us girl-women, cleat-clad and pulling up our hair in off-center ponytails. Sarah made my mom nervous—if ever I talked about her, mom would ask me how that nice boy Greg was. Greg was some band kid I'd kissed after a joint chorus-band concert because I liked how swollen his trumpet lips looked in the streetlights of the school parking lot. He'd been surprised and called me for three weeks after. On the phone, I made him laugh, but I didn't love him, and I didn't know that was enough reason not to talk. In high school, long after Greg was old news and James had come back after dropping out of college, Sarah was still around and mom had given up. Sarah had a girlfriend by then—Trina—and Sarah said we were best friends and I said yeah, the best. By then she was all frosted tips and glitter, like if Mark McGrath had birthed Athena at a Claire's. Trina was classic femme, brunette and buxom and brilliant, and for a minute I thought I loved her too, but then I realized I wished I was her, in Sarah's bed. They snuck around at first, but Sarah's parents were from San Francisco and caught on pretty quick. Trina's parents were just happy she wasn't hanging out with boys all the time, and I was their enthusiastic third wheel, cracking jokes in between sucking on my ringpop as we walked the mall and judged the artfulness of the window displays. We never kissed; I never told her how I felt.

In college I fell for Ibrahim, who had returned to school a horticulture enthusiast after a Kibbutz-stay the summer between his junior and senior year. I was a freshman self-medicating my depression by plunging my hands deep in the community garden, volunteering for a seniors group to keep away the dread of my completely opaque future. I wanted to be wrinkled and in a wheelchair with the bulk of my decisions behind me, and because fast forward was not an option, I planted tomatoes for Greta and watched Ibrahim tending his garden in the sun. We didn't date long, but the days we had together streamed into too-late nights in corners of the campus library, before retreating to my dorm, where we would become a tangle of limbs and blankets solving immigration issues and questioning gender expectations beneath the soft glow of the white Christmas lights I'd strung along the ceiling. Hubris and youth. We broke up without fanfare; he had places to disappear into and I had too much to grow out of. I didn't know I was sad about it until I saw he had married years later, and I felt a flash of another life, ungiven, pass across my mind's eye. But it would not have been good.

I am always a spy as I stir the batter for a cake, throw a party, attend a concert, wondering, is this what is fun? Add Lex, add Leroy, Cecilia, add

Yvonne, add Claire, add any of my loves, add the harsh sensation of a body tired, add sleep deprivation, take away money, silence anxiety, forget the future, let the past and the now collapse, bake at 350 degrees for an hour and cool in the early morning, just before the sun heats the world. I am more a vampire of sensation than a lover or friend. C'est la vie.

Winter comes hard. I hear through the grapevine that Lex is dating a woman Claire hooked up with three years ago. Alicia? Something like that. Starts with an A. Or an M. Maybe Maura? I should know, but I have been trying not to pay too much attention when I hear Lex's name slice through the din of regular conversation. I've gotten into a livable routine with my heart good and quarantined. It's close to Valentine's and the Saturdays are long. Trish throws her letter jacket on my seat at Cubby and we have a couple beers before bouncing to a cigar bar farther south. She lights her cigar slowly, twirling it like a jewel between her fingers. I am more bluster and puff with mine, coughing when I inhale too deeply to get the nugget lit. Heady, I say, and laugh, and we clink amber glasses and let the smoke talk for us until our mouths are soft with tobacco. The room is low-lit with dark paneling and the music is from another era: a little swing, a little sad.

Sister's getting married, says Trish. To a dude? I ask. Yup, she says. Practically gonna be a family reunion in Atlanta. I know that's where she's from, but she doesn't talk about it much. We all suspect there was too much Jesus back home to make her feel welcome.

Do your parents like him? I ask. Well enough, she says, he's a good Kappa. Got a job with Lockheed right outta school. Fuck, I should've been an engineer, I say. Never too late, says Trish. Don't think I could focus enough, I lie, because being an engineer is just one of those early-adulthood different-paths that I put into a bucket of better-finances-but-likely-less-satisfaction for myself long ago. What's your undergrad in? I ask, realizing we've never really discussed it. Biology, she says. And women's anatomy, she laughs. You serious? I crack. Honorary doctorate, she smiles. You're a goddamn inspiration, I say and we order fries and pick at them between puffs and showmanship.

Trish and I met back when I was temping at the Food Bank, inexplicably located by Wall Street and full of earnest and anxious do-gooders. She was the only person who could keep a meeting from lasting an hour and unlike her peers, she never acted like she was looking for a political campaign to hop on at the first chance. One evening after I'd moved on to a better-paying gig uptown, I saw her nursing an after-work beer at Cubby, alone, and I took the chance to introduce myself. We ended up getting smashed and deciding the night needed popcorn and a movie. Never dated, but we'd been friends ever since.

She leaves when the tall drink of water she's been bedding for two months hovers outside the window a little after 1 a.m. I settle up what's left of the bill with my good credit and the cash she drops on the way out. A night wind hits me as I step outside and I pull my scarf up over my nose. I smell like leather ottomans and British libraries and gray-haired men in smoking jackets as I slosh towards the subway. It's warm underground and reeks of rotten piss, expensive perfume, and someone else's body. No cell signal.

On the 2, I fall asleep and wake up to a dude jacking off in front of me. I scoff at him and move and get off at the next stop and wish immediately that I had laughed or yelled or rebuffed him with my body or louder voice or something. I am shaking and embarrassed and I don't want to be embarrassed, but I don't want anyone to see how afraid I am, that I am so scared, that I feel so small, that I can't wait to get back to my apartment. He had knobby hands. His penis was blunt and veiny. His jacket was brown.

At home I take a shower and wash my hair and body three times. I dry myself, slowly—I am trying to be so nice to myself, I am trying to be my own antidote—I know my towel is my towel and these hands are my hands and this bathroom is my bathroom. The covers are warm around me and I pull them over my head, with my phone in my hands. It's after three in the morning. M's the only person I can think of who is still awake and who isn't Trish mid-fucking a gorgeous woman.

He's probably just getting home after his bar shift, I think, and so I call him—it's been years since I've called him, though we still text now and then—and he answers with kindness and a question in his hello.

Hey, I say, hey, I know it's been a while, but I'm a little freaked. Are you okay? he asks And I say, I guess, I don't know, this dude on the subway was just masturbating in front of me. Well, at least he wasn't doing worse, he says, and I say, yeah sorta. I wait a minute before I say anything else and he lets me wait a minute and we just breathe on the phone until I speak again: I gotta admit it's weird because I feel like he touched me, I say—it feels just like that. I feel so fucking violated. I'm sorry, he says. I'm sorry, that sucks, he says. And I'm mad that I don't know what to say next and so I just listen to him on the other end of the line and I hear him unlock his front door and walk in and so then I ask if his night was okay. Bunch of drunks, he says, as usual—I mean what're you gonna expect—and I am grateful for his voice, and that he is not the man on the subway and that I know him. Yeah, I say. You ever think you oughtta get back in construction? I ask. I don't know, he says. It's brutal work. The weariness of hitting forty is in his voice. Can I come over, I ask, and he asks, what about Lex? which I know he has been waiting to say because why am I calling him at all. I say it's over and I'm such a mess, and he is quiet again before he says, at last, text me when you get here.

I do and he lets me in and we fuck in his hall. I bite his lower lip and he grabs the back of my neck and looks at me and says: I am always missing you, and I say nothing and lean into him and he thrusts and thrusts and thrusts and I moan and we slow and then move quickly, together, before he pulls out, grimacing, to come on my stomach. His semen runs down my body and I set my foot on the ground. I kiss him. He smiles and traces the line of his cum with his finger. I go pee and wash up and then we gather my clothes and disappear into his room. We lie together and I tell him she's been gone for months. He says nothing. What the fuck is wrong with me? I whisper and hold my hand aloft, in front of our ceiling-staring faces, and he reaches up and traces the veins on my arm. You still love her is all, he says, and holds my hand and brings it back between us. I am tired and self-conscious, and I know he knows I have no argument. It's not convenient, I say. No, he says, it's not.

The next afternoon we're just waking up and I rise first and shower and put on my pants and shirt and everything and it still smells like cigars. He rolls over in bed and watches me dress. I lean over and touch his face and kiss him and tell him I don't want it to be years again between us and he says, we'll see. I have always been good at lying because the lies I tell are goals I haven't committed to. I miss him, even as I leave him, but I never say so, because I miss too many people and sometimes it is hard to tell if that's because I want one of them back or if I want a do-over with everyone.

Outside his apartment I take my silly grief into the city. (I have labeled it silly because I am tired of it, and it is easier to admit how sad I am if I call myself a fool.) The wind is cold. As I walk south down Broadway, the half-melted snow lines my route in gray, tar-fleck slush. I do not call anyone or text anyone. What can I say anyway, this obsessed wreck of a woman I have become? The patron didn't matter. Lex and I had been lovers and strangers and I knew about the impasse between us all along. A canyon of mystery. As I walk, a part of me still believes that I can hold out for her—the fates might slam us together. It had happened. It could happen again. She had arrived in my life, twice, unexpected.

I, or the city, swirls, and my vision blurs. You know she had (has?) such a sparkling laugh, so feminine and disarming from beneath those strong brows. I used to love to tease her and say outrageous things to get her laughing. Laughing at dinner, beside me on the plane, in our kitchen, on the street. Laughing, beneath me, again and again, as I kissed her and touched her and we rolled until she was above me and I was below, pulling her cunt to my face, slitted and warm on my mouth. Rocking, her hips, and I would lick, trace, lick in the tangle of her, feeling the quivering of her pelvis as I held her thighs and she rubbed against my flattened tongue slow and slow and slow and then harder and faster and then crying out above me. We would collapse in the bed with her sleeping and me staring at the back of her head in wonder, this woman in my bed, as though mine.

For my birthday one year she gave me an abstract, huge—for your room, she said—and when I protested, saying that her art should be shown off, she said the best things about us are between us. I wanted to ask what else have you shared only with me? But I kept my wondering to myself, afraid to expose my insecurities. I know now that it was this very anxiety that magnified the intensity of us—without it I may have settled into a comfortable love and then—knowing how addicted I had become to the pull and tug—I would probably have become bored. It is a comedy, youth. Or at least infatuation is.

I duck into a bodega to buy some jalapeño potato chips and coffee. Warm those numb fingers. Post a pic of my haul on Instagram like I'm some kind of gourmand and then stand under the awning sipping and crunching as I watch people trudge and slip by in the cold wet. The traffic stops and goes at the intersection in front of me and a haggard man with a walker plunges into the intersection and then down into the subway, inexplicably alive and unfalling, in spite of nature, the concrete, this misery.

Men I have traveled with through time, but the women, even the girl-women, have been continents I inhabited. To break up, to split with a woman, is to be sent into exile. And to return is to re-enter a land familiar but changed. The warehouses have all become galleries. The gas stations are condos now, housing someone else. I recognize no street corners, except by their name.

I finish my coffee and go home. Another weekend, another month. It's all the same.

In May dad and Daniela show up, with warning, and I can tell that they've decided I'm their next project. It's obvious they've made their decision to fix me without any real commitment—they are only visiting for a week, after all—so the whole plan is really just an excuse to tell me what I should be doing with my life. This course correction begins, first, with rent, because mine is too expensive now, and dad says I should be looking for a studio and not be living in a big one-bedroom like this when it hasn't even been two of us for seven months. I tell him, fine, I'll look for something else after the lease is up. Daniela walks around my apartment with confusion and pity in her eyes, like how could anyone live like this on purpose, and I resent seeing my life through her eyes and I resent that anyone could believe, so utterly, that I had brought this mess on myself by not going gently into a good marriage, to a good man, in a good place, whatever good is.

Their presence exacerbated my loneliness; the self-blame I had begun entertaining with evening bottles of wine and long stints of drag show makeup tutorials on youtube was now a lovely snarl. Whose expectations was I living up to anymore? Did I even have any for myself? It was obvious I had failed the hopes of my parents, so sure of my success when I was young, so confused by my inability to just settle down (stay the same?) and get on track. Dad loved that phrase in particular, as though life were a series of railroad stations and trains that required, merely, a choice: A, C, 1 2 3, F, G, which train, which track, which destination? I wondered if he believed his wives were just different trains he was riding, hop-skipping from one to the other midlife like a kid jumping over platforms in the railyard. I took to following his conversation at a distance, alert to questions but ignoring the rest. Words, noise, and then, what do you think we should get for dinner? and I said what do you feel like? before Daniela interjected that she wanted Italian because we were in Brooklyn and so I said let's take a cab to L&B.

He got the chicken parmesan and she got the linguini with clams and I ate my lasagna slowly, watching the regulars in the room and wondering what secrets were in the walls. He's been talking about what he calls my difficulties in New York and says, it was just a phase, anyway, about Lex, and I say, why do we assume people have phases anyway, maybe everything that happens in people's lives is part of the same story. Maybe there are truths about people that are unexpected, and he interrupts and says is that it then, you're a full-on lesbian now? And I say, I'm bi, I was bi, and I'll be bi and then he says, you should just date boys then anyway, it's easier isn't it? And I say yeah, there are some things that are easier, like YOU, when I date boys, but there are other things that are not. Daniela holds his hand under the table and sips her water and then turns to me and says, you've changed your hair, and I say, my hair is the same, I just didn't blow-dry it, and she says they say your hair is the first thing strangers notice about you. And I say, oh, is it? and ask the waiter for another glass of wine.

There are three more days of similar conversations. At one point, when we are walking through the farmers market by the park, Daniela tells me I should really check out this other New York writer Jonathan Lethem because he writes about Brooklyn and then dad asks why can't I just bang out a nice YA trilogy if they're so formulaic and predictable. I say, I don't know, they don't really excite me, and then I say yeah, sure, I'll look into him (Lethem), because I have no interest in insulting these two people who are family, in the moment, when they are trying so hard to connect with me, however wrongly. Look at the size of those zucchinis, I say, and we buy strawberry hibiscus jam from a table stall because it is pretty.

On Sunday we go to MOMA, along with every other touring family, and I cross my arms and make myself small in the crowds, clocking favorite paintings like friends I've promised to have dinner with later in the week. Work is a vacation with built-in features like order and fakery; on Monday I enter the office delighted and Florida says she's never seen me so smiley. Our dollar store mogul boss regales us with his certainly undisputable genealogical connection to Thomas Jefferson (through his wife) and why the estate tax should be abolished ("it isn't fair to our nation's innovators"- LOL) before heading to Sotheby's to hide more of his fortune in a few paintings. Florida flips her hair and asks me if I can even imagine having that much money and I end that conversation quickly by saying yes, before leaving for lunch to keep myself from dropping Engels in the middle of the room. It's a testament to my cynicism that I assume Florida would look at me cross-eyed were I to start talking about why the rich are parasites and unworthy of our admiration, but the fact is that she loves royal gossip, and so I don't trust her.

When I get back to my desk, the Speaker of the House has left a message for XX the third and I've lost my morning shine. I slog through the day and retreat to Grand Central at six to pause, alone, amidst the hurried commuters passing beneath the painted constellations. Dad and Daniela meet me by the clock like they've promised and I get a shot of them—"in front of the Apple store," they insist—before we walk west to the Carnegie Deli and pay too much for our sandwiches. You know, this is where funny people of a certain age used to eat (I don't think the original even exists anymore). I am over the dream of New York because I know it is based on a city that only exists in movies and the newspapers of the past, but I cling to the romantic set-pieces of a bygone era when I am in front of tourists like my dad and Daniela as if my life's purpose depends on it. Dad says wow when they bring out the desserts and I know he is getting his money's worth—a hope fulfilled—while I smile and tally the hours until they leave for the airport.

Hug, kiss, goodbye, I love you, yes I'll visit soon, have a safe flight, text me when you get home, and schwoop they are gone into a taxi and I am untethered again, as anonymous in the city as a face in a discarded photograph. This is the heaven that celebrities lose after they've gained any notoriety; this is the precious gift of ordinary living in a place too large to keep track of your comings and goings. Usually I am thankful for the din, but after seeing my family, the taxis and pedestrians and other people with other purpose magnify my self-doubt: you're such a failure. You're such a coward. You're more risky than brave. You've accomplished nothing. You're not interesting—that's why Lex cheated on you. And then the better, kinder part of me offers grace: you're still young. What do you know about anything?

On my way to the subway I Tinder-swipe to a pretty face and text her to meet me Friday night at a dive in Brooklyn. She says she's in and I continue swiping, past Yvonne, past Trish—it's a small world even here—and then I switch to the men, where I am more selective and wary. Drinks planned for a bright face behind glasses, Tuesday evening. This is what passes for meaning, for now. I muse that the city is like a mistress that reminds you that you are alive; she never demands your consistency. I go home and get hammered and sleep.

6

Then—everything was different. After Yvonne got me a lead on a two-bedroom in Hudson Heights or whatever chi-chi (shee-shee?) name real estate agents call that fingerling part of Manhattan, I took the chance and moved. My roommate Jess was hardly ever home, and it felt like the neighborhood was leftover from a lost dream of the city. On Saturday afternoons I'd hear an opera singer practicing her arpeggios and arias and on other nights across the courtyard of our building a violinist would play scales before Paganini. I took my place as a bit player in the drama between our Albanian super and the Dominican super next door. They ribbed each other about whose sidewalk was cleaner, whose windows better kept. Both enjoyed catcalling me, and I laughed it off, even as I resented it. On the weekends I walked the streets anyway, deep into Fort Tryon and onward, to Inwood Hill, where the paths had been overtaken by brush and the street lamps stood broken and neglected amidst the trees. I listened for birds, kept going, until I popped out by the soccer fields and the stone that commemorates the Dutch theft of Manhattan from the Lenape long ago. Of course, the stone made the exchange sound much more like a purchase, like a good deal. I turned back. In Fort Tryon I watched Orthodox women promenade through the kempt flowers near the Cloisters and pause to smell them. Other times I disappeared inside, seeking quiet and cool stone and the chance to encounter something beautiful.

Under the vaulted ceilings I pretended at prayer, hoped awe could suffice for respect. The Romanesque corners and Gothic windows mixed together in stone strangeness, offering up an approximation of the sacred, with each element reassembled regardless of time or geographic origin. In the garden I mispronounced the names of herbs to myself and in the tapestry room I wondered at the mystery of the unicorn and what moralizing and mythological understandings once leapt from the threads. Every reliquary reminded me of my skulls, each a saint of death. What would it feel like to be so devoted? So hungry for oblivion?

When winter came, I walked through snow and wrapped my scarf around my neck to keep away the Hudson winds. Neighbors shuffled by, puffy jackets that had sprouted legs and walked off their department store racks, each only distinguished from another by their top-most adornment: bright knit caps or baseball hats or the occasional fedora. My frame disappeared into layers and layers of leggings, pants, shirts, sweaters, jackets, gloves, boots, scarves, and a variety of hats. But even then, the wind bit me. I did not go home for Christmas, but skyped with my mother from Starbucks. She was drinking eggnog. She said I was ungrateful. At the end of January I quit my job and drank too much wine again. It wasn't the first time I'd quit a job with just enough savings in the bank to cover three months, although the previous times I'd been fresh and less afraid of the consequences. This was desperate. Jumping from a burning building, all that. Sometimes you have to save your skin, especially if your skin is what's left of you. I knew my friends were worried about me.

I am in sweats and doing my best living-room imitation of Leslie Caron while watching *An American in Paris* when the rent-paying ghost comes in and drops her totebag and peels off her coat and says, whelp, I'm pregnant. The music continues and I shuffle around for the remote control to mute the trumpets and then look at her. Her stomach is its usual flat-ish shape. She appears no different, really. The same elegant fingers, short hair, and fitted cardigans.

Oh my god, I say. Yup, she says. I gesture for her to sit with me. I decide it is better not to make any statements, to stick to questions. How do you feel? I ask. I'm scared, she says. She starts crying.

What do you want to do? I ask. Like, about being pregnant? I don't know, I don't know, she says. I consider that this is only the second time I've sat with a friend as they cried for fear of a future they have not consented to, and I am grateful my webbed network of women have been so lucky. Jess, I will go with you, I say. Abortion or birth? she says, accusingly, because I can tell she feels alone in the prospect of either one. Whichever you choose, I say, and she collapses onto me, and I hug her and cry with her, because I hate that there is a man somewhere, who might be a father, who is not crying. She sits up and wipes her eyes.

I think I should call my mom, she says, scrolling through her phone impulsively, as though her mom was not on speed dial, as though she had to be found listed among the other names flashing before her eyes. Of course, I say, because I know that other people can take comfort in their parents, and I know that this is what she needs. If I have to go home, I promise I'll find a subletter, she says, and I say don't even worry about that right now, even though I am very worried about the prospect of more expenses before I have income again, and also a different future, undetermined, in which I live with a single mother and a child that is not, but still suddenly, my own. When she has retreated to her room and I am alone again, I pull out my computer and shoot ye olde temp agency an email. And I wait.

The day comes. I sit with the other plus ones in the waiting room at the Margaret Sanger center, behind the metal detectors and locked door, where we, the support network, wait for our friends/lovers/countrywomen to finish getting their pap smears, biopsies, checkups, and—for a few—abortions, before emerging from another locked door, so-kept so that we all have safety from harm. I am reading some Kate Millet, because it's overdue, and I should have read her a long time ago, and around me are brothers and lovers and friends of all genders and races, but mostly young, I guess. As I'm waiting, Lex walks in—fucking Lex—right there, and she doesn't see me yet as she kisses a young woman in white—so pregnant, I can see that, I can't believe that, and so much younger than us. I realize I am barely breathing, that I'm incredulous that her girlfriend (partner?) is having a baby, or maybe (?) she is just there like me, but no, no that kiss wasn't that sort of kiss. How fucking basic. Millet sits closed in my lap. I pull out my phone and text Cecilia. Lex is here. What? she texts back. Where is here? I'm waiting for Jess to get done, I say. Oh yeah, she says, and then, oh wait is Lex getting a checkup or something? And I say, no, fuck, she just kissed a pregnant woman. Oh shit, says Cecilia, I heard she was dating this real post-protestant girl, all fuck-religion but still into being a mommy. WTF, I text, because this is easier than looking up, because I can tell Lex has seen me, and knows that I know she is there. She moves to sit closer to me and I put my phone away.

I'm not here with my girlfriend, I say, and then feel dumb, but I've said it and I can't take it back. Me either, she says, and suddenly my worst thing is the perfect thing, and I'm glad. I just assumed, I say, and she says, it probably seems that way because we did date, but just for a minute. Ah, I say, and wonder why she is there, but instead of asking I say that I am supporting my roommate. Where are you living these days? she asks me and we catch up, and it isn't weird, and I don't know what to do with this ease, so unanticipated after these many months, now years. We stick to the easy subjects that run from our mouths to avoid the subjects we are not speaking about. Yes, I say, I like it up there, when she says my neighborhood is alright, and then she tells me she has moved back to the Lower East Side. I'm not surprised, because of course she has. Yes, I say. I'm down there sometimes. She smiles. We sit in silence for a bit, and the door opens, but it isn't Jess and it isn't her ex, and a guy gets up to walk out with the young woman who has just emerged, full of smiles and carrying a brown paper bag—no doubt—of contraceptives. I glance at Lex. She looks mostly the same, save a few new lines around her eyes, just little threads of leftover joy, and I wonder about what makes her smile these days. I want to see you again, she says, and it is direct and without confusion. I think that would be nice, I say. Because I am afraid to tell her I have missed her, and afraid that I will get what I have wanted and be heartbroken all over again.

I'm not painting, she says. Why not? I say. Too busy with work? Apparently I'm good at selling art, she says. Of course, I say, and nod, because that is the way of it—finding a niche inside of a niche and losing a dream along the way. You? she asks, and I say I'm here and there, like always. I quit my job, I say, so I should be writing more, but I've been watching more Netflix than anything. She nods, and I am embarrassed that I am not more accomplished, but she doesn't look at me like the fool I feel. I've been temping again, I offer, and she says, all my favorite people are always temping. I laugh. I guess some of us aren't made for any one role, really, I say. She says I think you're right. Her face is flushed, and her eyebrows are raised in a flirtatious arch. I don't know what is supposed to happen next, or how long Jess will be on the other side of the door, so I just go ahead and ask if she's free to hang out later this month and she says yeah, I like the sound of that (like we might be friends or something, really, friends, that's what we should be). We both pull out our phones and scroll through memes and pictures and pithy platitudes and then Jess does come out, and she is smiling too, and I get up and tell Lex, I'll text you, and she says don't be shy, and we leave.

It is still winter, and so Jess wrap-zips before hitting the sidewalk and I tuck my scarf into my jacket and shove my hands into my pockets. The wind hits hard when we cross Bleeker Street and Jess says she wants to swing by the drug store to grab some ibuprofen before going home. Just cramps, she says, and I wait for more, but she is silent during the subway ride back. The apartment is warm from the hissing radiator and I strip off my outer layers until I'm just in my hoodie and jeans. After Jess changes out of her pants and into sweats, she joins me in the living room and her face looks aglow, the shadow gone from behind her eyes. It didn't feel great, she says, and I say it was so much faster than I expected. They told me if I'd been a hair earlier I wouldn't even have had to have a procedure—they could have just given me a pill—but in some ways I think it is better this way? Quicker? she says. One of my friends took the pill and she says the cramps and blood were awful. I don't know. I think I just liked being there surrounded by women, she says, and I imagine how much different that must be than being alone in a bathroom, staring into a toilet bowl full of your unborn blood.

Let's get Chinese, I say, and she orders moo shu pork and I order Singapore-style noodles, and we gorge ourselves and watch *I Am Love.* God, to be Tilda Swinton, I say, and she laughs and says she's the only actress she's ever seen who can make her teeth act, and I laugh too, and say that's the best thing I've heard all year.

A couple weeks later, Lex meets me on a Saturday afternoon at George's Pizzeria on 181st—the last of the great slices left in the city. We squeeze inside and listen while the gambino crowd from Jersey joshes with George, now white-haired and aproned like Mr. Hooper from my childhood. They are broad and taller than us and dressed in long black coats that hide whatever's underneath. I feel like I've stumbled into a pre-code crime drama, but everything is in color and Lex looks like she's from the future. She's wearing a seventies puffy vest on top of her camo jacket and has her hands tucked into the front of her low-slung jeans like just her fingertips are frigid in the early spring cool. She's pulled her beanie back off the front of her shaved head and the dark hairs on her scalp stand at attention. The men tip their hats as they leave, folded slices in hand, and Lex does the reverse-nod, chin up and a dose of street respect. They're unfazed and get into double-parked black SUVs out front, headed to midtown no doubt, maybe the city offices (if the rumors are to be believed). George offers us garlic knots while we wait and we lean against the wall, making small talk about how we can't believe it's not warmer as he ribs his new hire—wouldn't know good pizza if it hit'm in the face—and I can't believe this place still exists, or that Lex and I are trying to be friends.

We walk and talk towards the park. A few families pass us, and one of the children is laughing and running with a balloon tied to his wrist. We see couples walking dogs. We finish our pizza. She asks me how the temping is going; I tell her it is as fine as it ever was, no better. I'm tired, I say, and we both know I don't mean tired because it's been a shit day or tired because the work is hard, but tired because I just don't want to put on the armor today, check my back, squint at my future. How do you keep at it so 100, I ask her, and she says, I don't know, stuff like this. Good gallery parties. Being quiet in my room.

You ever go to shows anymore, I ask, and the night we met feels three lifetimes ago, and she says yeah, I do, in fact there's one tonight if you want to go, and I say where and she says Bushwick (of course). The building's not up to code, she says. One of those. (We don't know how afraid we should be; it is before the warehouse disaster in Oakland, and we are yet fearless.) And so when we finish our walk near the highest point of Manhattan, we take the subway rattle-crashing underground, under the river, farther east, until it is night and we are more at ease and unwilling to act like this is new.

I am still tired, but I feel, for a moment, like I am living. By the door, a skinny tatted white girl with green bangs and black hair is stamping hands. Five bucks, she says, and we fork over the cash, plus some change just to unload. We walk in as though entering a cave to some dark heaven. The light is red and the walls are graffitied. We follow the trailing kids and black-clad aging roadies into a square warehouse space with six jerry-rigged bunks lofted around the ceiling. At least one is occupied. A few spotlights hang by haphazardly placed staples and binder clips from a pallet-rack two feet below the ceiling and the stage has been built where a kitchen once stood. The microwave is still stage left. I clock that the exit is also the in and it doesn't take much imagination to come up with reasons why this small room might get too full too soon, but right now I am in it, and so is Lex, and we're both on the back wall, yelling light conversation over the pre-music-music while we watch the first band set up. They're a hardcore group from Detroit, and I realize all of us are older than we used to be. While I'm telling Lex that Leroy's doing the night shift at a hotel these days, one of her exes comes up in a crop top holding hands with one of those guys who is just there when there's a there to be filled.

How's it going Rip, she says, and I realize this must be Renée, mizz-post-protestant, the one I thought the pregnant one was at Planned Parenthood but wasn't. She's skinnier than I imagined, and coifed and striped and painted like a high school detention reject whose limited idea of rebellion came off the rack at Hot Topic. She should be in a mall in Connecticut somewhere, but instead she's a walking example of Lex's democratic tastes, and her boyfriend stands beside her, unaware how interchangeable his American Gothic frown is with a different unhappy-but-willing dude. I know I'm staring, but Lex is casually catching up, and Rip's fish-pucker mouth has its appeal. I can't believe I ran into you like this, she says, and I look at her neck and wonder what her hair looked like before the ends were dyed pink. This is V, says Lex, yelling, and then she leans in a little, and I see for a second their chemistry: Rip's blatant hunger, her eager attraction as shiny as the saliva on her lick-bit lips.

They say more, but I've stopped listening. The band is setting up by the microwave and the drummer is one of those guys whose hair never quite gets long enough to pull back but is also somehow never short enough to not be in the way. He's fiddling with his set while the bassist and guitarist run cords from amps and plugs to microphones and their instruments before squatting and strumming and fiddling with dials to test the muffled moan of their soon squalling. They're all white—maybe the bassist has a dash of Persian—but then a keyboardist, unexpected, shows up and he's Indian and I realize they're all childhood friends. What's the band again, I ask Lex, interrupting whatever she was saying to the ex and her male accessory and she's like, I don't know, Kierkegaard? And I say that sounds about right, and the room is getting crowded with a younger crowd of disillusioned masses. Finally Rip leaves.

I've heard they're good, says Lex, nodding towards the stage, and I note the way the lead points at the others while he's giving directions, pick in hand, and I figure that's as good an indication as any of the quality of what will come.

What that is: loud, an assault of sound, but that is to be expected these days, and I tease from the noise a sure tenor, wailing high amidst the drums and filler guitar. They jump in hard and the amps are worn with a beating midrange like a snare dampened by too many towels. By the second banger there is no room left, not to stand, not to think, not to feel, and the people surge together with the wrangling front man, his grandfather's hours on the assembly line as near to us as the smoke-hard grunt of the room's howling. What is worn ironically among us is ambition; what is concomitant is the surety of our imposture, imposters, in the darkness, and I smile at the wood-hung ceiling, and I forget I should still be nervous about the night. The sound is getting heavier and their faces wild. Lex has given over to it, like I never got to see her be that first night in Portland, and I marvel at how we have changed in the interim. I want to drink the air. My ears are ringing.

We leave halfway through the second set and walk towards the river, but we're too far in, and so we grab one of the black towncars circling after a drop and get the Haitian driver to take us under the bridge, where the Pillar spews its patrons into the night like so much chewed up-gristle. When we get there I beeline for the bathroom and find a decidedly underage crowd mixing bottled vodka with koolaid in a handicap stall. I piss and leave, say nothing, join Lex, and we do shots. She says the thing about this new gig is how fucking gross it is the way they want to buy the fruit of someone else's risk, they just want to consume everything without tasting it, she says, and we get beerbacks to wash down the sting.

When my eyes start to swim, we get up to leave and just outside the front door some of the koolaid kids call her a faggot. She turns and says dyke to you, and one of the kids rushes her like he's gonna hit her, but she squares up and pops him right in the eye before he knows she's done it. When he hits the cement his friends come next and I'm grabbing the ones I can catch by the scruff of their hoodies and she's fending off what she can. I hear more than one punch land and I hear her groan and the whole thing is a bloody scramble. When I finally get a break and can get a look at her, she's on the ground and stumbling up and I'm screaming and there's a gash on her forehead and a slice under her left eye and it's already swelling. I grab her and we run, run so hard we can't breathe, until we are up the hill and among the stores and bar patrons of other bars, and then we're doubled over, panting, and I puke. She's leaning against the wall and some girl sees us as she comes out to get her rideshare and says omg are you okay, and I say can you just get us a car, and she says yes, and so we get in. I say drop us at the subway, but Lex says no, I'll pay for it, and we ride back to my place in silence.

In the morning I wake up and we're both in bed, bruised and feeling like hellspit. You look like a rotten pumpkin, I say, and her head's still on the pillow with a bag of frozen peas beside her just like we drifted off. She tries to smile. There's blood on my pillow and her teeth are black-streaked from it. Shit, my hand is fucked, I say, and I get up and wash the cuts that've dried and get a warm rag and some ibuprofen to bring back to her. She takes them carefully and then I leave again to get a glass of water. She swallows the ibuprofen like a pro and I sit beside her and clean her face, slowly, with the rag, trying to figure out what is a cut and what is just blood. When the painkillers are good and working, she grins, then, with her dark teeth and tells me I look like shit, and I smile and say if I look like shit then she looks like last week's trash. Yesterday was a good day, she says, and I fold the rag to a clean side and say you've got a funny definition of good.

Maybe if it were a different year, or if I'd had a different feeling, I would have kissed her, but this morning I know it isn't the time, and so I daub at her puffy skin and wish for a different world. She says that I'm pretty ace at the motherly thing. Do you remember in Portland, she says, that one night we saw some white dudes kicking some other white dude on the ground and you called the cops as we walked away? Yeah, I say, because I remember thinking how dumb they were. How if you really wanted to kick the shit out of someone you'd do it in a back yard, or in a house, where no one else could see. She says to me she's been through some shit, but it always seemed like the kids wouldn't do stuff like this, right? But they did, she says. It was just some fucking kids.

I don't know about the kids, I say. To myself I think about how I don't know that I ever thought the kids would get it better than the olds, or that the world is really moving forward. I hear people talk about progress like time or people or culture are always getting better, but the churn feels like the ocean and I've watched the waves enough to know that they reclaim as much as they give. I've always admired your optimism, I say, and when Jess wakes up and finds us watching reruns of *The L-Word* in the living room, we pause and tell the story of what happened. We tell it again when we are at Cubbyhole the next Friday and Yvonne and Cecilia are shaking their heads and saying they're glad we're okay, and we tell it again to each other at a late-night diner over waffles, and then again, drunk in the summer evening. We tell it until we know every play, until the blood doesn't hurt anymore, until the scar becomes a hero's weapon, and we share the secret language of that night like a brand on our hearts' guts.

As before, but somehow not as before, she is my occupation. I learn the stupid trivia I should have learned on other mornings: her favorite color? turquoise. Her favorite song? doesn't believe in such a thing. Her favorite time of day? evening. Her favorite drink? a stout, room temperature like they serve it across the sea. Her favorite place in the city? Greenwood Cemetery, where she sits on weekend blankets like a Civil War spectator, listening for the murmurs of ghosts. I haunt her. I expect her. I notice the roundness of her tongue, still in her mouth when she is thinking. I see the lines of her knuckles and wonder at what her hands will hold before the end. She does not stop me from watching, from being near, and why would she—who doesn't want to be seen so closely, with such joy?

One Sunday in July she's waiting for me at the Museum of the Moving Image in Queens and I've forgotten, because I'm in bed with another woman—Alexei—and my phone is off while we spend the hours in sex and conversation. When the sky is already gray-black with night, I turn on my phone and get Lex's texts all at the same time, then voicemails, until she stops, sometime after 3 p.m., with a pissed message about how I should be more respectful of other people's time—she's got shit to do, she reminds me—and even though I call her then, we do not speak for a month. Alexei fills the gap with stories about Cyprus and I play with the cascading immensity of her Greek hair, and by the time I call Lex again, I have forgotten that she was as mad as she was and that it used to hurt when I heard her hello. It's evening and I am standing in Union Square, watching a one-footed pigeon pirate walk across the stone. Lex! I say, and she asks how I've been, and I say good, fine, I met someone, and she says she's glad, but she isn't, and if she had been in front of me, she would have bitten her lip—she might even be biting her lip even as she speaks—and I apologize, for what it's worth.

What does that even mean? she asks, and I say I guess it means I know I fucked up and I know this isn't enough to make amends. Okay, she says, and for a minute, I wonder if I should even be this sorry, but I don't think about it again until she asks if I want to meet up in Central Park on a lazy Saturday afternoon. I see her come across the lawn with a blanket under one arm and a basket in the other and I realize, predictable irony of ironies, that she is in love with me, maybe for the first time, now that I have Alexei and I am never calling. We have missed each other like trains passing to the destination the other has just left. Her busted eye has healed into a crescent scar and she has shaved her thighs recently—them, strong and exposed as she folds and sits beside me. I check myself and the same attraction is there, but the sensation I ID is lust—devoid of its previous vulnerability. She asks about Alexei and I say that she tastes like licorice, and Lex laughs and says she knew a girl, once, who smelled like high school. She wear that citrusy drugstore perfume? I ask and Lex says she must've, but it was also her sweat, so like the girls Lex used to finger in the bathroom between classes. I bet you had so many secret admirers back then, I say, and Lex says she wouldn't know. I had such a crush on this teacher, she said, one of our regular substitutes. She looked like the woman every

Geena Davis character is based on. God, I say, no wonder. We eat and watch a contact juggler wriggling like an upright snake on the lawn. You know, we could get married now, she jokes, and I look away and am suddenly, briefly, tired of her.

I thought you didn't believe in marriage, I say, and she says, I must have said that a long time ago. You did, I say. And you? she asks. I think it's good that it's the law now, I say. But do you think you'll ever get married? she asks and I tell her I really don't know.

Fresh goosebumps emerge on her wind-kissed skin. I wait. I expect to feel heartsick, but instead I am full of the knowledge of her, and the memories of what we have lived through, and that feels like enough. I read this article recently, she starts, and I say yes? And she says it was about how the moon was formed—they don't even know really, she says. They don't know if it was formed because of some big collision or if it co-evolved, or if earth's gravity just sucked it in when it was passing by. Am I the moon in this scenario? I laugh, and she says no, the moon is the moon, but maybe you're right about why some people come and go.

Alexei was a tease and I didn't care if I had a type. We didn't say I love you but when we were naked she whispered, I want to belong to you, and when we were clothed, we argued about bagels. It was very New York. She was from Astoria, knew every side street, every pothole. When she was little, she played under the table in the kitchen of her dad's taverna while he barked at the sous chef and cooks. To the public, her mother was the hostess, but to the restaurant, she was the boss. If she walked back of house, the world stopped, she told me. She tasted everything. The best compliment you could get was her smile. I cried into my plate when Alexei made me grilled octopus and then stood by to watch me eat. They taste like sin, she said, because we have no right to eat them—they're too smart.

The days I wasn't with her I liked thinking about the next time I would see her, and when we were together it was easy to pass the time. She was forthcoming in every way that Lex was not. She told me about her first love (a girl in third grade, she swore), her homophobic grandmother, her reoccurring dreams (two: naked on the subway, flying over the ocean), and what she wanted to be when she grew up (an elderly style icon). My dad wanted a boy, she explained about her name. She didn't doubt herself; she didn't try to make life more than what it was. My various anxieties, for a moment, were forgotten, and I succumbed to the charm of her enthusiasm. We fucked in lazy mornings and fucked in midnight fury. We fucked when we felt blah. We fucked when we were happy.

When she told me off-handedly one evening about this guy she had hooked up with over the weekend, I dropped my fork. I had no idea she was bi—that had never been mentioned—but it also felt supremely silly that this fact surprised (or floored?) me at all. They'd met on a kink site. He was okay, she said, but you should have seen his abs. I got the impression she wanted me to join in a kind of mutual appreciation of how beautiful he was, but I was too upset to do it.

I thought you knew I'm not monogamous, she said, and I said I thought that meant we weren't monogamous YET, and she said no, she was bi AND poly and I said, shit. I stared at the dust flying through the sunstreak beside our table. I'm not poly, I said. I'm so sorry, she said, I thought I'd been clearer than I guess I was. Are we done? she asked, and I said I didn't know.

To prove to myself that I could (maybe) handle a poly relationship, I hit Tinder and okcupid over the weekend until I caught a bottle of wine and a French lay, but he sent me a dick pic the next morning (ugh) and none of the women messaged me back. I didn't want to meet them anyway. I wanted her, only, and suddenly that was a problem.

A couple weeks later Alexei and I are still trying at whatever we are that we won't let die and she takes me to this underground gambling hall behind a medical supply shop in her (my once) old neighborhood in Queens. She's wearing a dress that fits too easy and winking at me when the men flirt with her. I take her home again. It goes well, our pawing, our furtive rocking, but I can't help that my daydreaming about us has been replaced by jealousy. I know I have to end it.

I never liked her, says Lex about Alexei, the next time we meet up, and the sound of her voice echoes in the hall of broken statues at the MET. You never met her, I say, and Lex says she knew enough. It's not like you to forget plans, anyway, she says, and I say we all make mistakes. Was she even at the level of a mistake, though? she asks and I say I harbor no ill will towards her. I wish her well.

We stare at the pointed marble breasts of a Greek idol and I remember that time Alexei traced her finger down my stomach and told me about how everyone thinks the statues are white and so tasteful, but that actually they used to be painted teal and mustard and magenta. We laughed at the thought, tangled in our togetherness. Alexei told me these statues used to look like casino decorations, I say, and Lex says she isn't surprised.

We walk to the period rooms with their silken walls; we stop and stare at the curling Mayan glyphs amongst the gold; we stand askance of the Papua New Guinean wood men. As we leave, Lex asks me how my mother is and I say I wouldn't know. I haven't heard from her in a while. Doesn't that worry you? she asks. And I say, it's been peaceful. And then I say, I guess it should, but I don't want it to. Your mom's unhappiness is so exhausting, she says. All mothers are exhausting, I say. Maybe so, she says, and I know she's humoring me. A taxi honks nearby and the traffic hums and stops with the lights along the avenue.

Why did it take so long for your mom to leave your dad, I ask? and she says money, and then she says, no. She says: I think mom just thought that's how men are. It's hard to imagine you having parents, I say. Really? she asks and I say yes. Let's go to Julius, she says and I turn and hail a taxi.

7

We were all inside the house. Gere was beside me, but he was just James and just visiting, and I could tell from his breath that he'd spiked his orange juice with vodka. It was Christmas morning. Gran had been gone for years now. Dad yelled from the bedroom to go check the cinnamon rolls and Gere looked at me like fuck if I do, so I did. They were the refrigerator kind that come in a tube with icing for when they're done, plump like freckled, dead caterpillars. I had graduated high school and was enrolled at PSU, but I was gunning for Lewis & Clark or Reed, as though a transfer might be the answer to my freshman year anxieties. It didn't help that I came home every weekend. It didn't help that I was trying on self-hate like a good goth lipstick job. No school friends. One study partner—a girl-woman just as unsure of herself as I was, but blonder, and prone to throwing herself at boys when drunk. I was jealous of her recklessness; I was afraid of what I might become. A month earlier I'd run into my English T.A. on campus and he had remembered my name and he'd said V, you have your own drummer, don't you, and I'd rolled my eyes and said yeah, I've read Thoreau too. I didn't know (should I have known?) he would try to kiss me in February after we got drinks after class. I would kiss him back and I wouldn't regret it, but later I would wonder if that meant I was dumber than I liked to think.

But at Christmas he was a boring T.A. I barely knew and my family was the familiar, predictable shitshow I wish I didn't. Mom came in, wearing a dress that was much nicer than the morning called for, and she stopped in the middle of the living room, but I could see the movement of her—I knew this was a pause and not a join. She said, I'm leaving your father and I can't do this, I can't do this today, and I saw tears on her face, and I got up to hug her but she waved me away. Then she was out the door. James looked at me and I looked at James. I went looking for Dad, and I found him in the bedroom sitting on the edge of the bed and scratching his beard while he stared at the wall. He frightened me in his immovability, but I didn't want to ask him what had happened yet, because I didn't want to hear anything he had to say. I turned around and passed James in the living room and went to the kitchen and pulled the cinnamon rolls out of the oven. I iced them, and while I iced them, I wished that Dad, or James, would come in, but they stayed away, and so I left too. Mom had taken her car, a blue civic I would have preferred as my getaway, but Dad's white 86 Buick was sitting there like a holiday float—god he was so cheap—and so I hopped in, grabbed the thin, hard steering wheel, and decided to make my own fun.

I failed. Turns out driving west for a few hours on Christmas in Oregon means rain to snow, light to dark, and an even closer loneliness. At the coast I turned around without touching sand or sea. White snowflakes swirled and dropped in the light of my highbeams. I sat forward and close to the windshield, so nervous of the elk that could emerge swift and monstrous from the black-green treeline. I pretended like I knew where mom had gone, or what her reasons were, but then I'd remember how little she offered to us—ever had—and I wondered, like always, who she had hoped to be when she was a girl. The house was dark when I entered it. I got undressed and brushed my teeth and listened for signs of life. Then a snort came down the hall, and a squeak of the mattress, and I knew at least that my father was there and sleeping, restless.

The next day it wasn't Christmas anymore, and as we congregated at the kitchen table with coffee, I asked if there was bread, and dad said yes, and so I made toast, while he and James sat together in silence. Is that it, then? I asked. And dad said what do you mean? And I said, we're not going to talk about her being gone? And James said, it's not like she's dead. And dad said, what do you want to know?

Did she say anything to you? I asked, and he said, obliquely, I don't think your mother ever wanted to be married. Why did you marry her? I asked, and he said because he didn't know what else to do. That's a shitty reason, interjected James, and dad said, no doubt you'll make some mistakes in your life too. Why didn't you leave, then? I asked. And I watched him, and I saw the tomato sauce stain on his robe and I saw the wear of his slippers and I thought of inertia, and how he seemed to have made all of his decisions years before. I had a few affairs too, he said. But you didn't leave, I said. I don't know, V, he said. I think I liked coming home. I guess I always hoped your mother would eventually like that too. She didn't even like gardening, I said, almost to myself. James got up and got more coffee and bumped me out of the way. I didn't care. I had always known that his unconscious cruelties were not personal; I was annoying, like the morning sun, bright and inevitable. I stared at the Garfield tshirt he was wearing as he sat back down. It reminded me of when we were kids, sorting through seashells on the coastline, looking for tiny spindles and small conches. Mom would say she was going for a walk and we wouldn't see her for an hour. Maybe she had always been leaving. Maybe the day she left was really the end of something she began before I was born.

She didn't resurface for another six months. By then I was on summer break and working at Best Buy to save money for a hoped-for week in

Europe. It didn't happen. She called because she needed money, and for the first time in my life, I had money to give. Just two months, she said, and that's how I learned she was drinking more and avoiding the question of new employment. Her first escape job lasted five months. Will you go back to waitressing, I asked? (I didn't have it in me to help her pay for her life for long.)

Together, my mother and father had seemed so middle class, so sitcom-solid. On her own, my mother was precarious. The money I gave was a temporary bandaid, and soon a parade of white knights followed behind me, getting her to the next month, the next year. Mom and I only talked, sporadically, then, when she was manic and sure of what the next year would bring. Via email I heard from Dad that the divorce was final. Fine, I thought. Fine.

We were supposed to be friends and it was supposed be over, but Lex had been beautiful and butch in the bar, and she had touched my knee under the table when we rolled our eyes at the music choices of the frats in the back booth and I had found myself watching her jaw, and lips, in the dim light. She had seen me watching what I saw, and so I had gone home with her. To her new apartment, more empty in its spaciousness and more full of unseen money. Someone else's paintings propped against the wall—her own work, where? Gone, hidden, stopped. She had one rug—ragtied—and a wire-and-wood table. After decades of being cramped, Lex filled the new space like Julie Andrews spinning in the hilltops. Blankets flung on furniture that didn't seem finished. Used dishes left about. Shoes kicked off, creating divergent pathways between and around the furniture. There were no doors. The bathtub stood across from the bed, askew from the kitchen counter. Her shoes were already gone, I realized, drop-slipped sometime since entering. She poured water from a water jar in her refrigerator. The whole setup seemed European to my untraveled eyes and I liked the idea of it and I liked the idea of us in it, right now. She drank and I watched. Even though I could see that we had grown older—her in this new space, eyes dark-lined and scar-set above strong cheekbones, her still-shorn hair—our history kept us young. It was magic that she could break my heart twice and I could stand here, poorer than her, and yet in this moment somehow more powerful. I had something she wanted. I was something she wanted. She permitted me this. She inhabited this room, one we could have only imagined years ago, with absolute ownership, and I watched her move in it. She watched me watch her. She leaned against the counter. She waited for me and I made her wait.

And then I did not.

So I shouldn't have been there, but I was, when I woke and lay across her body to check my phone, and it shouldn't have been her who saw me stare at the message from my dad, but it was; she was the one who heard me say, that's it then, and when she asked, that's what? and I said she was right about my mom, that I should have been worried, it was she who knew. She held me as I cried, so full of hatred and love and relief and loss, and she did not let go as the radiator hissed and I did not want to leave. She didn't ask me to, for days (how many?) until I did, finally, for Portland—alone, with the dead before me.

Let's pretend I loved my mother, pure and without complication. With that feeling, I would have arrived and seen Brent—yes, that was it—and he would have hugged me beside baggage claim and told me how they had found her body in the living room on the couch, upright, with a needle in her arm. He would have told me and I would have collapsed and gripped the patterned rug and felt the earth shifting under me, without certainty or future, and I would have wondered who I was. With that feeling, I would have wished for a graveside and a chance to visit, and the entire trip I would have showered and dressed and walked with the fog of loss in my every breath. I imagined this scenario on the plane, as the earth of America changed color and elevation below me. I stared at the patterned clouds and wondered if I, then, were in the heaven that the ancients had imagined, and I thought of how empty it was, and pristine. My mother was not there. She was not where I was going, either, but I was going to say goodbye, anyway.

At the airport, Brent picked me up at arrivals and we said hello. He asked me if I was okay staying at my mother's apartment—the rent is paid through the end of the month—and of course you can take anything you want. I said yes.

I couldn't remember why I had believed that Brent would let me crash on his couch. I don't know why I hadn't made other plans.

He hands me the apartment keys and says okay, here you go, and I sit in the passenger seat and he drives. I do not ask him if he was using heroin too. I ask him later when she first shot up and he would say last year and he would say: with me. They had been intermittent lovers most of my life, but sitting in the car, and even after, he is a stranger to me. I have seen him enough times to recognize that he has aged into that taut middle age so frequently worn by addicts. The pudginess of his youth has diminished from chronic dehydration, lack of sleep, and the blasé living of opioids. I hate him, but I hate him less than my mother, because he is just a phantom, and she had been mine, or at least familiar, at home.

He pulls up in front of her apartment building and I am glad that I can't see her front door yet and I am glad that he doesn't wait for me to go in. I walk around the side and use the hard key in my hand and I walk in and it smells like her. Like Dove soap and cigarettes, bleach and something else I've never been able to name. The couch shows no signs of what happened there. Brent or the coroner or whoever does these things must have had enough foresight to clean up whatever mess she left—I was already thinking about it too much. I didn't want to imagine her neck slack, her head rolled, her jaw open, her eyes wide, her body so relaxed, so dead. It was a grotesque end to a small life, I thought, I think, and as I stand only feet from where it occurred, I want most to be back in New York, buying coffee and jaywalking through streets. I'm staying in her apartment, I text Lex, and she writes back, simply, FUCK.

There is still a little food in the fridge—frozen lasagna, old mayonnaise, rotten limes. Microwave is broken. The lasagna takes an hour in the oven, but that's how it goes. I turn on the tv and it is the usual school shootings and celebrity in-fighting. I turn it off. Lex told me two nights before, when I was sitting in my underwear and a tank with my legs tucked under me on her couch, that the grieving was worse if the person was someone you resented. That there was no peace to it, just time, and jesus we don't know how to talk about death very well anyway. I texted her again and then regretted it. I said: God I wish you were here. It was true and not. The fuck else was I supposed to say? Probably nothing. Saying nothing was frequently better than anything at all.

I jammed my phone in between the couch cushions and decided to make the space clean, as clean as an altar. The impulse was an exorcism. I found Comet under the sink in the bathroom and a gallon of bleach in the kitchen cabinet. Scrub, swipe, rub, buff. Two water-damaged issues of Vogue on her coffee table—into the trash. Black mold on the windows—wiped in gray streaks on the panes until I folded the rag again, scrubbed, and watched the dankness of Portland disappear under my fingers. The bathroom had been forgotten long enough for soap scum to rim the tub and bits of her hair to cling in spirals on every surface. A single strand flashed in the light as I held it between my fingers and marveled at our shared vanities. My mother had styled her hair with precision, like a better hairdo could change the tenor of a year. She had straightened, stretched, sprayed, set. I knew the same routine, practiced and perfected by years of experimentation: add volumizers, heat shield creams, blow dry, twist, hairspray. She commanded her hair with the control I wished she could have saved for other choices. The humidity was a formidable opponent. In the bathroom I sat amongst her filth on the cold tile floor and screamed and then cried. I leaned against the mildewed shower curtain. I hated her so much. I loved her. I hated her so much. Bleach fumes stung my eyes.

It was after I saw that Lex had not texted me back and after I'd satiated myself, temporarily, with the heavy warmth of lasagna, that I found a heavy suitcase in my mother's closet, behind a pile of her shoes. Unreasonably, I had begun rummaging through her stuff with the faith that

I could find some essential sameness between us. The suitcase offered a piece, or rather many pieces of this unsolved puzzle, but they completed nothing. Found: a stash of unused needles, cravenly sequestered in a felt bag—a jewelry pouch she had probably plucked from the bins of the Goodwill outlet in Sellwood. Beneath it were pictures of white men I had never met, and several of her mother when young—she who I didn't really know. Here she was by the pool, dressed in a striped suit with her hair close-cropped and curled. There, she watched my mother swimming in a yellow bathing cap as a little girl. Elsewhere, she holds a glass of something clear, in a pine straw back yard. Her husband, so withered by the time I was a baby, is pointing out his handiwork at the base of the fence posts. Mom had not yet been born. I flipped through time. I saw weddings—my father, mother in Portland—and her mother's, in Bend. The veil is the same.

Do you Sharon, take Michael? Do you, Michael?—you know the Methodists say will you, not do, said my mother, once to my father. I must have been fourteen or fifteen. It must have been dinner. Do you hear that, V? Will you. Gran's influence left a burn. And Margot's left a veil. James was not there.

I dig further: opera gloves and a fur hat, a hat pin and a strand of fake pearls. I had never seen her wear any of them. Beneath a bandana I find a stack of drawings that James and I had made as children. She saved more crayon drawings than paintings, more scribbled notebook paper notes than later renderings. I find this as endearing as I am disturbed; it was easier to love us when we were fresh. Tucked in the back pocket of the suitcase there is a note from someone named Thomas. They had been high school classmates, I surmise, and at some point in the last fifteen years, he had loved her.

It was ludicrous to want more from these artifacts, but I did. I wanted explanations. I wanted answers. We were a small, forgettable people with middling opinions and predictable escapes. This shouldn't be so hard. But she had taken refuge away from life until life had left her. Her memories were now nonsense without context, precious solely because she had made them so, and I had no place for her things because I did not know her reasons. I would never understand her context. I threw almost everything in the trash with the dirty rags I had used to clean the bathroom and the hair swirls I had plucked from the tile. The pictures I kept. And a few of the drawings.

Gere called me in the morning and then picked me up as if we had planned to meet up as soon as we had heard. He was in street clothes and had let his hair grow a bit. I hugged him, and he was smaller than I remembered. The drive was quiet. At the mortuary he told me he would really appreciate it if I called him Vivaan and stopped calling him Richard Gere and I said, but what good is enlightenment if it doesn't change you?

He didn't like that much. There was a wait to pick up mom's ashes—I had no idea that was even a thing that could happen—and so I disappeared into the familiar halls I had walked with Leroy many years before. The dead were still the dead, with over a decade of new inhabitants amongst them. I traced the chiseled names on the headstones and enjoyed the cold of the stacked and orderly sarcophagi. An Irene, a Bruce. My mother would not be getting a place here. Her bone bits would be scattered. My tears started again like a spitting rain and I stayed among the departed until I realized it had been an hour and I had been gone a little too long.

Back at the front, Gere was playing candy crush on his cellphone and next to him on the bench was mom in a paper carton and white plastic bag. She had been reduced to late-night take-out. We gotta get an urn, I said, and he said they sell those too, and so I picked out a plain silver one, brushed chrome, and sat on the bench with it, empty in my hands. Okay, Vivaan, I said, gimme a hand here, and I popped off the top of the urn and he popped open the take-out box and poured her ashes and chunked bones into the new vessel, so-chosen because it seemed more important and respectful than leaving her where she was. She powdered the air as she fell, and I saw his eyes get hot and milky. I did not know what to say, and when he was done, I pushed the lid back on and slapped the top for good measure and we both waited a beat for the dust to settle. He brushed her from his knee and said, let's go get some Thai. As we left, he crushed the temporary bag and paper container into an overfull trashcan outside the door and I cradled the urn like a football. I waited to feel some kind of presence—ghostly? upsetting?—follow us as we drove in the city, but the day was the day and the urn was the urn and we were just the left behind.

At the restaurant I took her into lunch because it seemed rude to leave her on the floorboard of the car, and the urn stood tall on our table between us. He ordered pad thai, and I got the pad gra prow. How is New York? he asked. Okay, I said. And San Francisco? I asked. Shinier and shittier, he said. (Rishikesh, obviously, had not been as permanent as first planned.) I'm moving to Thailand next month, he said. What's there? I asked. An easier life, he said. Is that what you've been looking for? I asked. Why are you always so judgmental? he said. Should I have said that I'm excited for you? I asked. It would have been nicer, he said.

We ate stoically. He looked at the urn and then looked at me. You know one night, when I was in high school, she got drunk and made out with TJ, he said. I picked at my food. That's fucked up, I said. Yeah, he said. She just couldn't fucking cope (and I turned to look at the urn), could you? Vivaan James Gere looked startled. Let's be done, I said, I need to be done.

She hadn't left a will, and so, after a brief conferral, we decided to scatter her at

Multnomah Falls. Gere drove in silence. The Columbia River Valley opened itself in front of us like a beautiful wound, oozing beneath tree-lined hills and filtering clouds. When we arrived, I carried the leftovers of her across the parking lot and up the bridge and James waited for me while I held her under my arms. We stood a moment and watched the falling water and a few tourists pushed on around us. The falls were heavy with new rain and I knew it was pretty but I didn't care. I decided to get on with it. I pushed and tugged at the top of the urn but could not get a good grip. It stayed stuck. Can you help me? I asked, and Gere grabbed the top, while I held the bottom. It did not budge. He yanked harder, and I held tight, and nothing, and then he yanked again, and the urn slipped, lid on, and rolled casually off the bridge to the rushing water below. We turned and gripped the railing and watched it bob and knock as it traveled towards the culvert, hitting rocks along the way. Soon it disappeared, and she was gone. We stood there, staring at where she had floated away, and listened to the cascading water behind us.

Let's go, he finally said, and he drove me back to her apartment. I hugged him and we promised to stay in touch via email or something, both knowing we wouldn't. In her bed I binged Netflix and laughed and cried and then slept. By the time I got back to NYC, I'd already been in Portland too long. Grief hit me hard, though delayed, and I was a skeleton of sadness and frustration. My breath was short and my chest hurt in trembling ebbs and tides. I did not want her back, but I did not know what to do with the end of her. Each day was a litany of weird and uncomfortable silences, over-disclosure, and a fog between and in every thought. Nothing was without the taste of grief and everything was also colorless and void. I had become all reaction and hiding, like a lost wolf in a foreign land.

I did not tell Lex I was home. Or anyone. I made no plans. I got up, posted nothing, called no one, walked everywhere, waited for sound to hit me, smells to bring me back from the grave. Human piss. Sirens. Somehow everyone found out anyway. No doubt Cecilia heard from Yvonne from Trish from Lex . . . and then small gestures appeared—text message condolences, emails, gifs on my facebook feed, tumblr re-whatevers, snapchat sorrys. I responded to no one, devoured everything, stared madly at the incessant on and on as the SPAM and marketing emails piled up in my inbox amidst the failed human attempts at understanding. There was nothing in me to give. Weeks passed at a string of temp gigs in Midtown. It was not the first time I had been treated like so much furniture in a room full of men, but it was the first time I saw how foolish their clung-tight status made them. What tall children! What empty anxiety! I carried the weight of death in every water offered, in every clicked key. It felt dumb to be so sad. One meal a day was all I could stomach; I lost weight, looked better, wondered why we so idolized unhealth. I stared at the ceiling. I baked cookies that I did not eat. I read recipe books. I subscribed to new magazines. I ordered makeup online and waited for it to arrive.

Lex showed up on a Saturday afternoon, with a bottle of Nyquil and a bouquet of flowers. I didn't know if you were sleeping okay, she said. The apartment was not as much of a mess as it could have been, I reasoned, as I watched her see me, in this space again. Where's Jess? she asked and I said I didn't know, because the truth was I had been avoiding her, like all life, as if to admit someone would be to admit, more tangibly, that I too, was not also dead. She sat on the couch. I sat next to her, sorta, with my legs between us like a wall.

Would I have done more to reconcile with her then, if I had known how long it would be before we saw each other again? No, I conclude. Because I didn't have it in me to be an us, not with anyone, not then. I craved nothing. I wanted no one. The first tidal wave of need had broken into a new desert, and I was its territorial inhabitant. She was talking, I realized, and I said that I was sure it would get better with time. She rubbed my feet.

No echo of past lust, no fresh feeling grew between us. It was as if my interest in her had become the thing we both wished most to keep alive. Now gone, fled, who knew, to some inaccessible interior, there was nothing to share. I felt so guilty. She kissed me on the cheek as she left, said that she would be thinking of me—I should reach out when I was feeling up to it and we could talk—and I said thank you, and sounds good, and the door clicked behind her.

Later, I heard from Yvonne that Lex had met some famous writer at a coffee shop in SoHo. She was older, had a rescue dog. Briefly, they became one of those couples no one hears from, and it was better that way, at least for me. The sadness hummed behind my smiles. Numbness became a sensitivity that broke my ability to ignore bullshit. People merged into a great everyone, and I was apart, and unconcerned by daily anythings. I stopped going to Cubby for a while, drifted further into solitude. I know Cecilia and I did one-on-ones, but most of that spring and summer is forgotten now. Time lost to hurt, all edge without a handle. I woke up, briefly, when Claire called me crying—her mother had died too, heart attack—and we swam together, tiring, and wondered at the shore.

8

I first met Leroy in a sophomore seminar on Russian Literature and Orthodox Theology. Maybe the fact that we were the only two people in the class who found Florensky's doctrine of icons logically sound was the start of us, but to be honest, I do not remember. It seems as if we have always known each other, and I mistake that feeling for truth. When I remember us before, and younger, we were ever escaping. Dilapidated buildings, strange homes, old woods, high hills, cold ocean—we prayed for Bigfoot and hunted for ghosts. When we tired, we camped. When we got hungry, we ate roadside strawberries, glove-box jerky, and melted Snickers. When we got home, we told ourselves the stories of our adventures.

Now he has escaped for good, lost amidst the hardwoods and bent trees of the original Cherokee homeland, and he will not be drawn out. In letters, I hear of verdant springs and bone-chill winters. He knows the lambs bleating and the rustling of turkeys. We have diverged, but my heart aches for our former disappearances. With heavy mind, I pilgrimage to his door like a hopeful saint at the pillar of Simeon. He admits none of my New York affectations—"who do you think you are, sweetie?"—and I must come as meat, raw, and ready for appraisal. We walk the aisles of Ingles and select orange rolls for a late-night snack. We brew tea and wrap ourselves in mythical otherworlds. There are mug rings on the coffee table and the sofa has cat-scratched gashes along its side. A space heater zmmms beside us.

It's been so long since I've seen you happy, he says, and he is right, so I quit my job two weeks later—a form of self-care, of self-sabotage. Sometimes they are the same thing. I did not know my future would soon be thick with other people's disasters, myself a vortex amidst them. It was New Year's. I would run into Lex at Planned Parenthood three months later. We smoke a bowl and cross our legs together beneath a crocheted blanket. I read Ondaatje. He reads Stevens. Midnight comes with windy knocking and we sleep like this, entwined. The dogs bark into the treeline and I dream of snakes, like children, greeting me at the river. We treat morning as a slow sabbath and wander in the woods in the afternoon, as we are wont. There are many reasons why I love him, but perhaps, most, I love him for his quick remarks at the lesser, more prestigious paths we both did not follow—

"Lawyers have to love being right more than being surprised," "Academia is a fool's game; you've got better odds in Vegas," "I choose anonymity." I return to him again and again, sneaking away between my New York dramas as if to a better home. The leaves mark my arrival—green, then red, then gone. Of Lex, he takes to calling her Halley's Comet and I, like Twain, her celestial complement. We gossip and tell self-deprecating stories of our blunders in online dating. He burns sage and anoints my head. We read G.K. Chesterton aloud, then Seferis, then Morrison. Downtown one night we see a woman on a horse clomping down the avenue and we swear she is a phantom. At all hours we walk-speak our own magic and the air vibrates with possibility. Pause and smoke outside a shuttered bookstore. Watch the passersby. His laugh echoes off the cobblestones. We do not go to the Biltmore. What a mess.

Over drinks, one rainy New York evening, a mutual acquaintance from college tells me that she worries about him because he is not more ambitious; I say, why should he burn his life down for what he does not want? She says she can't imagine wanting what he has. I say he is happy. We drink and hug and part in the drizzle. I do not say he is smarter than everyone I know. I do not say: I miss him all the time.

When he visits me in New York, we walk the High Line and then secret ourselves in my kitchen, roasting chicken and drinking wine and doubling over at our own jokes. Charles and Jess join us and the evening turns into late-night pajamas and snacks and spliffs. I am the old-hearted woman of us, and I drift into napping as the conversation continues, then wake in the wee morning to laughter, to hearing them love each other with their stories. The next morning is slow and Charles kisses Leroy goodbye before returning to Brooklyn. I wonder why I have ever wanted my life to take a different shape, why I have ever felt a failure.

The year dips and rises with our departures and arrivals. When we are together, I am well. When we are apart, I am chasing that same feeling. It took me years to identify just what it was about our exchanges—and then I realized, beyond the love and affection: we enabled each other's freedom. We fed the best hidden parts in each other and reveled in the aesthetics of our liminal status, apart from every room, like only poor kids who have sat in college seminars can. In his eyes, none of my hi-low playing would ever be construed as evidence of unintelligence or ignorance. He gave me the only freedom worth having: the chance to make mistakes without judgment. And I, him. How cruel the outside world, tick-checking every wrong word, every choice that shows your class of origin or aspiration, and how gracious this simple love: an open door, a shared knowledge, and rest.

One summer night when we were living together in Queens, in my arms, Lex talked again about her mother being second-gen Mexican and her father third-gen German, and how they met at New York-Presbyterian when he had Lyme disease. We had spent the day touring and walking past the LES haunts of her childhood, now jam-packed with bars and boutiques for young white people who never would have stepped foot in the neighborhood when she was growing up. Back then everyone thought she was Puerto Rican, but she barely knew Spanish and came out so white it confused her abuela. I was more bruja than anything, she says, and she tells me she did not correct them their assumption. In the mornings, her mother lit the candles of saints and prayed, while Lex dressed and trudged to and from Catholic school. A woman's virtue is like a bucket of water that must be kept pure for her husband, they said, with the windows closed and the boys in another room. My teacher fucking said that, she says, and the evening breeze cools the sweat on my skin and she continues: here I am, trying to pee enough not to get a UTI every time my dad raped me. I listen again. Though she does not speak to him anymore, she speaks of him sometimes, like this, when the vault cracks in the afterglow of sex, and the earth permits all things. The close, dark past settles between us. I listen. We breathe.

She speaks with her head against my chest, staring elsewhere. Your stomach is gurgling, she says, and I run my hand over the textured smoothness of her shorn head.

Our room in Astoria had been a cocoon of togetherness, with the paraphernalia of our lives strewn across walls and in drawers like an explosion of what we thought domestic life should be. My notebooks stuffed in a drawer with our socks. Her paint brushes in bags under the bed. Canvases leaned against the wall. A smattering of my skulls on the windowsill. She expected healing; I expected safety. We gave each other neither; we were just people in love. The painting she had given me hung above the bed, and I kept it even after the breakup, fucked other women and men beneath its bright stripes, stared at it from my desk on other nights, three glasses of wine gone, remembering the quiet tiptoe of her as she crawled into bed, freshly showered, after another late night somewhere, and I never asked. Should I have asked? Why should I have believed that love meant belonging to anyone anyway? Wanting permitted so much.

She bought me a small rack of deer horns on ebay—said they were evidence of all the innocents I had slayed—and I hung it across from the front door. For her: a pressed twig of Queen Anne's lace that I laminated and trimmed to fit in her wallet. She slipped it behind her ID—to keep it close, she said. Maybe she carries it still. I do not know what she has carried from us into her other lives, or what she found precious amidst our tug of war. When she emails me links of articles now, I read them for clues and secret messages, but there is no hidden meaning. She knows me and so she sends me things she knows I would enjoy. That is all.

College was a good (and quick) four years in the early aughts where everyone treated knowledge as important, and then after that I worked a bunch and ignored the boomer insistence that from this hodge-podge I could somehow make a career. A few friends stuck around academia and ended up on food stamps with PhDs. Others joined the tech world and put on their rah-rah faces (I know a cult when I see one). For most of us, though, nothing stuck, and not because we didn't try. Contract this and that. Freelance hustle. Temp gigs. We made meaning from our non-work, Tuesday-Wednesday weekends, sometimes Saturday-Sunday too—snuck trips, late nights, sleepy conversations.

After I graduated, I didn't go to Europe like I had hoped, but I did go to the Tetons for a long weekend. At night I slept on the hard ground and listened for bears. None came. During the day I walked beside Jackson Lake and swam in Colter Bay. In the evening I drove to town as the sun set behind the mountains, and I slowed and stopped and watched the buffalo watching me. I texted Lex. We were in and outside of ourselves then, so young. I knew she needed space. I didn't know the end of us not long after would not be the end for sure. What I remember most: sitting in the woods with the sun passing over. The way a yellow flower bent in the wind. My own untethered waiting, and then delight, as I exhaled.

Back in Portland, Lex picked me up from the airport and we kissed and made a big deal of having been separated so long; she held my face in her hands and put my luggage in the trunk. We pantomimed what we thought missing looked like, what we thought love should be. Did you find what you were looking for? she asked and I said I wasn't looking for anything and that made things awkward. When we got back to our apartment it was clear she hadn't done much while I was gone and I wanted to be fine with it, but I was annoyed. The bed was unmade. The bathroom was dirty. Let's go out for dinner, she said, I want to hear all about everything, she said, and I said sure, and so we went out to a bar. I told her about the cold at night, and how ancient the earth felt even though the mountains were young, and I said I'd read a lot of Baldwin like I planned and then I asked what she had been up to. Ugh, trying to land a gallery show, she said, painting, the usual. She touched my thigh under the table and I inhaled sharply and forgot my annoyance and remembered I had missed her. Later, in bed in the dark, I found her with my mouth, and felt again that I was home.

Classes, more classes. Comparative literature this and that. Work-study at the library, running through the card catalog with my fingertips—

why don't you use the computer?—because this is erotic, I couldn't say. Putting the returned books back on the shelves and in the process discovering the limits of what I knew and would be able to know in one lifetime. I smelled the pages when no one was looking. I ran my fingers along the re-bound spines and slipped each book back on the shelf between two others with the same precision that I knew Lex's cunt. It was unreal to me that the solitude between shelves could be so maddening. Snuck in a corner to read, I would sneak away further still, to the basement bathrooms graffitied with paint and markers. There in the far stall I would touch myself to relieve the internal knotting, like a storm (how horny I always was when so young). Inhale, Lex? I would whisper, and she was not there, and my teeth jagged against the bathroom door. It occurred to me that I am filthy, that this is filthy, that I love being a little filthy.

Here is a thing that is true: I am older and I am remembering, but I am also that woman in that bathroom now, and I could swear, in my bones back then I knew the woman I have become. Some organ intuition, some electric suspicion was in me. I am not saying I knew the what of the future; but I knew the kernel of what in me would break the soil. Maybe identity is a tautology or maybe that is more true of time. I then and now; these grays, those first sunburns. And the core of it is this filthy pleasure, essential and enlivening. It is mine even until now, still.

I see her in the sanctuary, and unlike myself, she is not alone. It is evening at St. Patrick's and the tourists and faithful are milling along the stations of the cross as the priest intones for the beginning of Mass. I am not usually here, but it is the day after Trump's election, and I, like many, have found myself lost and seeking quarter. My temp gig at a hedge fund has dumped me in Midtown at 6:30 p.m. and I need warmth and something lovely. I have often wandered into these sacred spaces, seeking rest from the manic-moneyed world, but I have never before seen anyone I know. I suppose I should not be surprised that she is here—with her mother, I realize—on a day of mourning. There is a sadness beneath the buttresses, as the city inhales together, wondering what will come.

The tension of us makes her turn. She sees me and smiles. Says, ma, I want you to meet someone. They approach me in the aisle and we make quiet introductions as the service begins. Her mother is shorter, darker, a tad stouter too. Their faces share the same evasive smile and I wonder, after we have said our hellos, what she knows. I do not have to wonder long. After we sit she pats my leg and says, it's nice to put a face with a name. I blush. The priest begins a call and response—and also with you—and I find myself crying without really understanding why. The tension of the previous night has not dissipated, but there is a new humming, unexpected, and louder than the great disappointment I am carrying. She has seen me; I have been seen. When communion begins, I file in line behind them both, tall and awkward and unsure of how time has led to here. Suddenly before the priest, I cross my arms and he blesses me while the sacrament waits for more worthy mouths.

Afterwards we walk to the subway together and Lex hugs her mother, says good night, I love you, before we continue into the night. Why didn't we meet before? I ask, and she says that she has worked hard for her privacy. It isn't easy to draw boundaries with her and me living in the same city, she says. You and me were always such drama anyway, she says. I do not argue with her, because she is right, and I wish I had known better. How are you? she asks, and I tell her about this guy I've been seeing a few weeks. Met at the grocery store, I say. He's fifty-five. (I haven't felt much this year, I don't say.) Grave robber, she laughs, and I laugh too. Any money in it? she asks. Not a cent, I say. Just that good old dick. Like fine wine, I hear, she says. A better head on its shoulders, at least, I say. Yes, she says. It must be such a relief to be old.

Grab a drink with me? I ask and she says sure, and I say I know a place, and so I hail a cab and we head down to the bar and book to sip gin and smoke cigars and spend money in the soft red light of its neocolonial environs. Those monkeys are fucked up, she says, as she waves the flame off her match. The statuettes wear little tuxedos and stand at attention amidst the dusted liquor bottles. Along the bar sit a smattering of alpha men hiding their loneliness in impressions of idk, pick-a-Mamet schmuck and you wouldn't be far off. Women with long legs and secret childhoods lean over them to order drinks and a kind of dance begins. One or two of the men get a number, three or four of the women get drinks, and everyone passes another evening, relieved to have filled it with their hunting.

Alberto, who has been here who knows how long from El Salvador, mixes drinks and greases the conversation with easy talk about the weather. Regular patrons huddle together to avoid the newbies and the back table fills up with a smattering of someone's birthday friends. The bathroom line gets long. I lean into my second cocktail and settle in. You know I think I probably refreshed the Times website three thousand times, I say. She laughs. I don't know why but I think I knew, she says. He represents pure masculine power to them, and that's what they love.

We're such a specific kind of a fool, I say. Yes, she says, American exceptionalism makes us vulnerable. I tell her she should be running things. She says no one who's seen beyond the moat wants to live in the castle. Like the Yeats poem, I say. The very same, she says, and we click glasses.

Her hair is longer on top than it used to be, and it hangs above her forehead like a reverse wave, headed out to sea. Both sides are shaven. In the lowlight she's got a touch of femme about her, but not much. Beneath her blazer, I can still see the lines of her sharp shoulders, the slip-peek of her breastbone over the top of her shirt. When she gets hot and takes off her jacket I see the tips of her nipples tapping the fabric of her shirt, and I become nervous and clumsy, spilling what is left of my drink. No binder tonight. God, you can still get to me, I say, and she says we're star-crossed or something. That sounds like a lie, I say, but I am smiling. Alberto comes over and wipes up my mess with one smooth, toweled swoop. Another? he asks, and I look at her for a clue, and she says yes, two. We broke up, she says, and I nod, and know the older writer girlfriend (she of greater success) is gone.

Don't you have work tomorrow, I say, and she says she can roll in late. And you? she asks. Still temping, I say, but nothing lined up for the rest of the week. Just finished a reception bit at a hedge fund. Connecticut crowd? she asks, and I say, at least sixty percent. What does your old man think of your professional limbo? she asks. That I'm brave, I say. You're certainly something, she says. I finger the edge of my hair beside my shoulder. I should have been born rich, I say, and she says that I would have made such a good dilettante. Does one really need money for such pursuits? I ask, and she says I suppose not, just an unserious commitment. I laugh, and I love that I am laughing, and that we are here, too late on this weeknight after the election, in the womb-colored heart of Manhattan, and I have no idea of what is to come.

When she gets up to use the restroom, I watch the tumult of bodies pass and glance along the wall, here for a drink, out for a goodbye, and back again. The room is warm and my seat swivels with my happy swishing. I puff and shimmy, grabbing the bar with my small hands for balance, and then lean forward, taking my cigar out of my mouth, elbow on the bar. Drink up for a sip, lean back, puff, survey, pick with thumb and forefinger the small shards of tobacco trying to wedge their way into my teeth. The world outside has slipped into uncertainty, but we are holding fast in our nation of two. She returns and the night's remainder is a slow burn of cigar smoke, the doppler claptrap of men, and her perfect almond eyes.

We were married three weeks later, on a Friday, and the winter trees scratched at the sky. I have never been so sure.

PART 2

9

Lex, my wife—that's the word that gets used, though not by us, except when nothing else will make us known. Neither of us prefer it. A wife, wifey, wifed-up—we are neither, but we are married. I introduce her as Lex. She introduces me as V. We revel in depriving others of answers, categories, neat bows tied up with so little understanding. But we are happy to be wed.

I move in and fill the apartment with my collections. Books stacked on the floor and windowsill, old newspapers flagged for clipping that will never happen, my skulls—relegated to the strange space atop the kitchen cabinets. By the tub, I put a basket of my shampoos and washcloths, arranged as if for a guest. In the kitchen, a cracked bread bowl holds new bananas and apples. By the curtains, I install hang-ties to draw the drapes and let in the sun. One of our first weekends after the wedding, Lex buys a knocked-about chest of drawers from a vintage shop in the meatpacking district and picks up Egyptian cotton sheets from a boutique in SoHo. Back home, she insists on hanging the neon painting of our early romance—still bright, despite years in the sunlight of my old windows—front and center in the living room. It is unmissable, and we fuck under it like we had before, like we would again.

The apartment became ours and my day habits reshaped themselves to the neighborhood. I told myself the food cart across the street made the best ham egg and cheese in the city (it didn't) and the new-to-me streets grew in crisscrossed routes from the front door of our building. I walked with fresh eyes and re-learned the sidewalks. I had a new north. Jess emailed that she'd given up looking for a roommate and had invited her (boring-ass) boyfriend to move in. We kept saying we'd grab dinner at Kashkaval Garden or somewhere else in Midtown but it never happened. Eighteen months later they got married at City Hall and moved to Park Slope like people do, some people—

At night Lex and I listened to the city, safe in bed. A siren passed, and then another. Too recently two gay men had been shot in the Village. A trans woman had been beaten nearly to death in Brooklyn. Since the election, swastikas had begun appearing in Sharpie on the subway. The air was tense, and moments of togetherness felt precious and meaningful, like we could will a new world with our homebuilding. Lex drummed my side with her fingers and we spooned in the darkness. In all my Lex-y daydreaming, I had failed to imagine the context of our marriage, the city as it was now, the worries we now carried.

You're breathing fast, she said as we lay together, waiting for sleep. The curtains moved with a midnight summer breeze. I get scared sometimes, I said. The safety we took for granted at home felt like a thin illusion, soon to fall away. Already friends and neighbors were complying in advance—being careful with what they said, hiding the best parts of themselves. Almost everyone I knew carried an unseasoned, razor paranoia in their waking. I wanted to rage, stand proudly against the creeping authoritarianism that extended from Washington, but I took the coward's route. I dove into the twitterverse and other internet metaplaces to commune and rant. We knew it was not enough, that screaming in a barrel is an impotent match against martial brutality, but I think we hoped that someone was listening. If men could be radicalized in chat rooms, couldn't they also learn to love themselves and people not like them, somewhere on the web? Perhaps not. What power could we offer them? What other carrot could they want? Secrets felt necessary. The news reported dead Black children, defaced synagogues, torch-lit screaming white faces. Nowhere was immune. In the city, white men walked through the Village drunk with impunity, ever-ready with insults and hate speech hot on their tongues. We grew walls for skin. I fantasized about revenge. It was good I did not own a gun (I told myself, I told myself). I turned away from a public I no longer trusted and tuned myself to her.

We got here like this: I fucked the old man, and he was worshipful, and held my face in his hands as if I were a jewel, but I was animal, and crawling out of sadness, with blood between my legs and scars on my skin. I saw Lex again, after we shared cigars, and she did not touch me. We remembered years past, in Portland, and admitted, finally, the fears that had gone unspoken: I, that I would never really feel what it was like to love again (at least like I had that first time we had tried) and she, that she would never live up to the pressure she had invented for herself: to be better than anyone else at everything she attempted, to be richer than anyone she had known, to be notable. We assessed ourselves like cracked mirrors and determined we were both seeking an idea from our past rather than letting ourselves grow up and out into the future that was newly ours. I am shriveling, I said—and she said, you are a cactus under a bell jar—and I laughed, because she was right. I saw her again, and then again, because I texted her that I wanted to, and this time she grabbed me and we smashed into each other with every shard and thorn we had. It was real, and I cried as she kissed me, and she said, I don't care if I am ever famous, I just want you to know how much I have always loved you. We should buy suits, I said, and she said we should go to the courthouse, and so we did.

To the man, for whom I had carried a brief but flaming affection, I told the truth. I loved someone else. He took it well; it was better he had lived long enough to have learned that not everything, even between lovers, is personal. We drank bourbon together and I said goodbye to him and watched him hail a taxi to get away. At my apartment, I hid in my room before telling Jess: I'm so sorry, but I'm moving out at the end of the month. And I did, because the suits fit dapper and the trees blessed us and in a courthouse back room I married the woman who used to be the girl that I loved.

She stood in the park with my heart. She! Lex, my lovely, with sugar on her lips, held my hand as we walked to her apartment and my new home, bundled in coats over our clothes. For a week I had no temp work (the New Year was approaching), and I fell into a lovestruck reverie, inhabiting every room with myself, cautious and as excited as a recent convert in the house of god. I hid my astonishment at our togetherness with an over-enthusiasm for domesticity and slow evenings of snuggling. So when she said to me, you're breathing fast, it was after my re-entry into reality, after the inauguration, after months of hate crimes, and I was not faring well. I'm scared sometimes, too, she said, and her echo was a balm. The ground was shifting; we could either cling to its cracking or hold hands together and face what would come.

Cecilia texts me right after the wedding, asks if I know anybody looking for a place, and I text Trish because I remember her mentioning something about somebody looking for a spot on facebook a few weeks ago. Turns out that somebody is Trish's little sister, and February third, Cora moves in where Cecilia's Connecticut-graduated roommate had been. You can tell Cora and Trish are related by the way they move their hands, but Cora's high glam couldn't be more different from Trish's loc-topped tomboy. It's Saturday and I'm on the couch, eating potato chips with Trish and Cecilia while we make each other watch our favorite youtube videos. From here you can barely hear Cora in her room filming Instagram makeup tutorials punctuated by Solange lyrics and her own no-bullshit aesthetic. Trish says she's gonna start a side gig getting her sister sponsorships. Like as her manager? asks Cecilia, and Trish says that's the idea. Cecilia cues up a Vine compilation on youtube of dogs being ridiculous and I fall on the floor laughing at a dumbass Pekingese. Later we order pizza and talk smack about Paul Ryan and other boring politicians in between trying to decide what to watch next. Cora joins us in PJs when she's done and we all stay up late watching *The Incredibly True Adventure of Two Girls in*

Love for the hundredth time (but Cora's first!) until I decide to just stay over on the couch and Lex texts, yeah I wouldn't go out in this rain either.

A few months later Cora still isn't famous, but she's had enough invites on podcasts and beauty blogs and whatnot that she lands a dece gig at Condé Nast. We meet for celebratory drinks and Lex shows up late with a toast full of congratulations and a warning not to turn into one of those Condé Nastys. We laugh and Cora shouts, no chance. Trish has this new girl, Heather-from-Dallas, and she says it isn't serious but everyone can see how smitten she is. Heather's light-skinned and half-Jewish and works in finance and we've got a pool going that they'll be hitched by next Christmas. Claire won't go in on it though, says she doesn't see Trish as the marrying kind, but then she raises her glass and gestures at Lex across the table—of course we didn't think you were either. The remark gets lost, but I hold onto it, pissed, and wonder what kind that makes me. I know it's only a joke, right? A joke—one of those jokes that gets repeated without thinking—as though we are all following a script someone else wrote a long time ago. And it makes me mad that we, here, these (mostly) queer women are not outside the habit of repeating, ad nauseum, the stereotypes we claim to shirk. Fucking hell.

From across the table, Cecilia sees me fuming—I hate that she can read my face so well—and comes over with ciders and asks Claire to scoot, says she wants to catch up with her spy friend. I'm a spy now? I say, and she says the quiet one is always the spy. Claire doesn't mind—she's been eyeballing a bicurious woman on a date with the kind of guy you pick up on Tinder and leave on the corner, and I see her stake out the territory next to them and begin to scope the conversation for the right move. The guy doesn't know his girl is already breathing heavy because the woman she's been eyeballing is now standing right behind her, but that's the way of it. He'll go to the restroom, they'll leave. He'll be mad-sad and then Tinder someone else.

Do you think you'll get married, I ask Cecilia, and she says she doesn't want to. I think I'm one of those committed spinsters, she says, even when I'm serious with someone. I like my space. Don't really want to play my music quieter. Don't really want to come home at a decent hour. Is that a part of marriage? I ask. Naw, she says, but it does seem like a lot of marrieds like it. True, true. Lex is talking to one of Cora's straight girlfriends and I can tell the youngster is having one of those a-ha moments that'll only really make sense to her in six years when she drunkenly kisses another friend and then doesn't stop, and it gets awkward, and she looks in the mirror and asks the right question. I've been trying to remix this Sylvan Esso album, says Cecilia, but it just sounds like Feist at a rave. I have no idea what you're talking about, I say, but

I look up the band from my borrowed desk at work the next day, and I text her: you're right.

On the way home Lex has her city shoulders on, broad and standoff strong, and we ride the subway in silence, my hand tucked into her arm, and the clatter of the train car dadunging through the underground. Cora looked happy, she says, as we enter the apartment. Do you really think Trish is gonna marry that new girl? I ask. No, says Lex, and then says she doesn't think it'll end well. Why do you say that? I ask. Heather strikes me as an opportunist, says Lex, the kind that opportunes to the coolest person in the room. And she can get away with it because she's hot enough, I say. Exactamo, says Lex. Fuck, I say. You ever think about hooking up with Trish? asks Lex, left field. Not really, I say. We never vibed, I guess? I don't know, she and Cecilia have always been so dece to me. They're more like sister-family now. I've always envied you, them, says Lex. I'm not as good at keeping up with people as you are. Yeah, but you're better at attracting them, I say. She smiles. Don't think I don't still see, I say—you make people forget who they thought they were.

She leans in and kisses me a thank you and her mouth smells like a split of fresh earth I could slip into and be forgotten. I turn away, embarrassed by my own intensity. Shit, I'm thirsty, I say, and get myself a glass of water. She claims first shower and I stand in the kitchen, drinking slowly, disbelieving that I am married, while the splashes and knocks of her echo back again.

We were all inside the house. I, on the floor, and my grandmother calling to me, her knees swollen and peeking from the hem of her calico dress. Breasts soft and enormous and her lip delicately haired. How perfect the shag orange carpeting seemed, then, like them all, undated, and me with no purpose but life. My mother was so young—I recall smoke, between her fingers—it was the beginning of her habit, yes—and my father settled on the couch, watching the news. He was in lumber—"a good industry"—and we ate, had a roof, got new shoes when school started and had cable for a few years. Later, when my mother left, he burned everything of hers from his life. The ashes sat in the fireplace until spring.

James comes in with his cars, smashbanging them across the longhaired rug and I am laughing and laughing. Swoop, and the perspective shifts: I am in a lap and hugged. Mom tickles me and I see my grandmother frown—you will make her soil herself, she says, no doubt, or at least she said something similar—she never did like my mother. Thought her too hard.

James comes over and bops my nose. Will she ever get big enough to play with? he asks, and my mom says: she is big enough now. Redeposited on the ground, toy car in hand, I vroom vroom along the floor, oblivious to him. No! Play with me! he yells. The car gets forgotten and I walk-stumble to the swollen knee. Bebop from lap to lap. He hits me. I bite his arm. We are put in timeout.

Later: my mother whips the gravy in the pan with a fork, smashing bits of flour to hasten their dissolve. Her hair is up with pins, and she is wearing a flat denim apron over her pleated shorts, long to the knee. Toes lost in slippers. Hair on her legs. Goddamn it, she says, and throws the fork in the sink. Grabs a whisk. I hate gravy, she says, and stares at me with green eyes, and I am not sure it is the gravy we are talking about, but I say me too! and she laughs and I laugh with her, so little, my little laughter, in my high chair.

She screams for James to help her. Come here, she says, and he sulks in, sliding his feet along the floor. Set the table, she says, and he obliges. Like this, she says, showing him where the forks and knives and spoons go. Gran will join us too. Then dad, bustling, union pin on his lapel. Maybe that night we ate Salisbury Steak with bird nests—English peas in mashed potatoes with gravy on everything. Maybe it was roasted chicken. She was a domestic reluctantress, succeeding, for a time, at keeping herself and us alive. For one year, when I was half-time in preschool, she ironed our napkins while Sally Jesse Raphael talked in the background. Phil Donahue sometimes too. Then Oprah. They could not save her.

I temped for years. The work? Easy. But the lack of money made life hard. I was offered a couple longer-term desks, but I didn't want to give up the delusion that this phase of life, this non-career-career really was only temporary. In every office I was an interloper. Each desk a mirror of its usual occupant. At one: a smattering of smiling strangers taped to the wall, ziploc bags of tea, hand lotion, an envelope of saved concert tickets. At another: nine highlighters and a selection of blue and black pens, beside them a cup of perfectly sharpened pencils. Here a drawer of makeup and hairspray, overdue library books, and file folders in disarray, there an odd action figure and wad of plastic bags, some tums, and a roll of paper towels. The executives I assisted were confident of their importance, but they were as ubiquitous as the concrete. It was the women and men whose chairs I borrowed, for a time, that I loved. Their worry hung on the handset of every phone. Lex called them "the absent" and I called them Cary, Jen, Jonathan, Shane, Thomas, Sylvia, Brian, please see the attached phone sheet for yesterday's / last week's calls.

They were an army of invisibles, and I was invisible amongst them. The parameters were clear: not too butch (male or female), add a dash of vocal fry, and on Fridays, an eagerness to gossip. For my part, I was the right kind of (com)pliant—open-faced with an easy hello. The right skin, build, comportment to pass as one of them, fresh and on my way, with just enough optimism to ease the awkward guilt of VPs and C-somethings who both craved and resented lowliness—you're a temp, sure, but only temporarily so, yes? Surely my story had a happy ending. Surely some nice man would buy me a great big house or maybe I would be snatched up by some conglomerate and be offered a better salary, better life, better future. I could hear the absolute meritocracy in their voices as they condescended to "see" me, passing through, passing so well among them as their best idea of a pleasant white woman answering the phone.

I held them in contempt for their unimaginative cosmologies. I despised them for their self-protective classism. They believed me theirs, by race, by class, by right, as someone safe, even as I held tight to the benefits of my invisibility—access, ease, rent. The fuck else was I supposed to do? Get on board? I was not a true believer. From where I stood, the prize looked rotten. I saw too closely how money twisted the blessed into slaves of material maintenance, suspicious of their family members and friends and expecting always a kindness to come with an ask, and an ask to come with a mountain of obligation.

Still, we lived most days surrounded by them, in their homes and apartments and restaurants. Lex's position garnered invitations to their parties the way Ivy League degrees confer legitimacy on strivers who would otherwise be non-existent to the unimaginative and arbitrarily moneyed of Manhattan. Or London. Or Los

Angeles. Or San Francisco. Pick a place. It was a trial to hear them fancy themselves so progressive for liking us. But we showed up. We attended their parties and openings and shows and weddings and we ate and laughed and dressed better, were more knowledgeable than any of them. Lex said I could hold a grudge harder than by all accounts my grandmother had been able to scowl, and I told her that was the highest compliment I had ever received.

Us! We are married(!); there is this us and I still cannot believe it. I was, suddenly, because of our marriage, better roofed, better insured. Lex's big time hit me sideways and made me antsy. I went inward, looking for my skull in the mirror and remembering the vibrating urgency of other evenings, so coolly at ease in my dicey independence (this, I re-imagine now—how palpable, no doubt, was the worry, then? or not. or not.). But together, married, Lex and I were stable. This I told myself.

One late winter evening I come in late, with soft-light eyes blurred by too much wine gulletted at an after-work soiree. I find Lex in the living room with the sofa and chairs pushed against the walls. Her errant flop of hair is pinned back and she has laid a heavy dropcloth on the floor. She scuffles in bare paint-splattered feet across its folds, moving between a nearer and farther vantage. A gallery-sized canvas leans semi-upright before her and the colors are a mix of muted blues and pastel grays interrupted by oversaturated red, teal, and yellow. She is not done. I couldn't not do it anymore, she says, unturning, as I walk in. Did you quit your job? I ask. Not yet, she says. I am going to say that is a good thing, I answer. But you don't mean it? she says. Good is relative, I say. She paints a solid black line across the middle of the chaos and then cocks her head cattywampus to judge it. I feel like I'm being used by everyone, she says, instead of using my life for us. I mean, this apartment is pretty baller, I say. She laughs, your place in Portland was such a death trap. I specialize in death traps, I say, and we smile.

She doesn't let it go. On slow evenings we talk about the west coast, wish for more sun, think about L.A. I've always loved palm trees, she says, and I tell her they were imported from Hawaii as a marketing gimmick. How American, she says.

The idea becomes a plan. Then: we pack. New York City, morphed into a shellacked version of its former glory, has become all high-rise apartments and empty storefronts, subway delays and shopping malls. It's a punchline of a faded dream, and we do not have enough patience to attenuate our stay with nostalgia. We hug our friends' necks and promise to visit and leave.

We knew California was not an escape—more like a wait-and-see—but the state line feels like the door to a golden citadel when we cross it. We breathe more deeply, unaware we inhaled shallow and short through the stark sand landscape of the empty west. L.A. was not a perfect refuge; greed was here, interspersed amidst homeless encampments and abandoned film scripts, but the light was dazzling along the sidewalk and it felt good to be a stranger. Anonymity cradled me as I had not known it since I first entered New York.

As is to be expected, the urgency of money determined our first three months. On my resume I said I was a freelancer—it was not the first time I had used this code to cover my years of temping—and Lex went through a litany of interviews she had lined up before we had even arrived. I knew she would slot in better than my own awkward jobbing. She, at least, had a series of titles and over a decade that could be verified and background-checked and admired.

I told my father, when he called to ask if we needed anything, that we had already found an apartment, even as we spent those first three nights at a Motel 6 out in Clairmont. What cash we had saved we coveted, nibbling on grocery store takeout in our room and scanning apartment websites for anything reasonable. I wanted to be near the subway—she wanted an assigned parking space. It was imperative we did not land somewhere with the same outsized rent we had abandoned; who knew when I would find work again? The uncertainty sent Lex into spirals of anxiety. Over the years her what-may-come attitude had been replaced by an accustomed comfort, while my own expectations of stability had slowly eroded. As little as I had to offer, this temperament was my best gift. I talked her through every freakout. She paid for dinner.

And we did find a spot—in Koreatown. It suited us like expats who have sought a different world to end the sting of their own otherness at home. When we wanted, we traveled to Silverlake and the cultural embrace of a more visible queer community, but in the evenings, we stayed in, and we opened our windows to let the breeze cool our hands over clinking silverware. We called it home.

Back east, Washington continued its erosion. The earth wept. Children—named Carlos, named Jesus, named Maria, named Valeria—cried in cages behind walls somewhere near us, walls that had been Wal-Marts, warehouses. When we were kids, fear-mongering chain emails warned us against windowless vans where we might be kidnapped; in our adulthoods the real threat was faceless architecture, so chosen to obscure its function as a variety of private prisons for infants and toddlers. We protested, as we had done against the war in Iraq years before, and I was ashamed that we were so untouched by these worst atrocities, until Lex yelled at me one night: it is our duty to thrive. We can't let them take our joy. Cowering is the first step to servility. We half-ass started learning Spanish, then decided to give as much money to Raices as our budgets could handle. Wildfires raged. I read Hannah Arendt. We shook our heads. We didn't know what to say. Our fucking felt political. Our laughter barbed. My muscles tensed and I moved through public space watching and listening for bad signs—dead birds, squashed snakes, day-black sky. I saw men on scooters. I saw the bus come and go. Life continued and children died.

On television, the press secretary's scorn was as palpable to me as the pursed lips of my grandmother on her worst and cruelest days. The news was a flagellation. I drew boundaries: consume the news by reading only (no tv news, no CNN, no CSPAN). When I was not looping on Russia, or abortion rights, or police brutality, or hate crimes, or the appointment of queer-hating judges, I opted to disappear, retreating into bouts of silence, my first and last refuge.

We bought a beater Volvo on Craigslist and I drove it north through the scorched earth, let my mind get distracted by birds, watched the side of the road for coyotes. I wanted a sign; I expected extinction. It did not come.

10

We were all inside the house. Dan Rather read the news. We were a CBS family, the same as we were Wendy's people (not McDonald's) and bought Charmin, Comet cleaner, and Clorox for the bathroom. James was in sweats and I was in a long night shirt. Both of us had developed the frequent habit of coming home and taking a shower immediately after dinner, if not before—as if we could wash the day off our skin, or deeper.

Our father lingered in his work clothes and his formality set him apart as he sat in his chair, eating a post-dinner bowl of cereal. (To tide me over until the morning, he would say.) Our grandmother preferred NBC, and Tom Brokaw's severe side-part, and so she would stay in her room and watch the world apart from us. Our mother did not like this nightly ritual. She would disappear, put on her nightclothes, and walk through the living room only to pause and remark on whatever upsetting headline could be gleaned, temporarily, from the top stories. Every now and again, cigarette in hand, she would sit with us. Then, she said nothing. A shook head, maybe a nod. Her cigarette would ash into an orange tray on the coffee table and I would watch them each watching the television. Gere-still-James might tease me, say something gross about Clarence Thomas, or crack a joke about revenge of the killer tomatoes. I would smile if he was funnyish or scowl in response. Locktite like gran-spite was his favorite twofer.

I never came out to them, but they guessed. Mom knew how I felt about Sarah before I did, but still I dated enough boys over the years to reassure (confuse?) her. Bisexuality wasn't on the radar—it was a whisper, the vibration of a string strung between two coffee cans, a conversation between two hapless friends. That Gere exclusively dated Black and Japanese women passed unnoticed by our family as a preference; they were hardly ever brought to the house. Maybe he was ashamed of us. It is hard to understand what he thought of our family. Were we ever an us? A mixed lot, perhaps. Five strangers beneath a roof. I am a citizen of the world, he declared on a summer afternoon, before leaving for a mandatory defensive driving class. What world? I thought. This is Oregon. What do we know about the world?

Our grandmother shuffled into the room in her slippers declaring she was hungry on her way to the kitchen. She ate pickles from the jar and once I caught her standing with a bag of uncooked hot dogs, about to eat one cold. Let me fry it up for you, I said, and she shrugged and watched me while I watched the sizzling pan. She was bored with life; it was obvious in every spent word. We gave her books of crossword puzzles for Christmas and she pretended like she liked them. Her nightstand was full of used tissues and butterscotch that rotted her dentures and irritated her gums. Piles of dog-eared *Reader's Digest*s and random issues of *US Weekly*. She knew more about Jennifer Aniston's love-life than my mother's past, although as I say that, I realize we all did (with the exception, perhaps, of my father).

In hypothetical daydreams I have often wondered what my grandmother would have thought of Lex—so "boyish" she would say, no doubt. Or: is this your friend? My friend. My iterant madness. She never spoke of our father's father, though they were married for fourteen years before he died of a heart attack on a plain evening. Dad preferred the twentieth century script: he was a hard man, prone to fits of rage. What manner of hurt did those words elide? Had his father given his mother the scar on her left shoulder, tough amidst her fragile and veiny skin? Had he destroyed the photographs from Dad's childhood? Why were we so without antecedent?

Aqui, Lex's mother said, outside the hospital where she met Lex's father when we were all in Brooklyn together, in spring, before we went west. I watched Lex, but she did not stiffen. She had lived with the reality of her father's violence and brutal ownership longer than I. Every story shocked me: when he was raping me I used to imagine I had seven sisters—after my ankle healed from him stomping it—when he left to live with his other family—I do not expect her to love him. She does not expect me to understand. I'm glad he's dying, she says, and her mother crosses herself but does not protest. Maybe she is glad too.

Dad joins us in the kitchen, says, Mom you can't live on hotdogs and candy. She says she can't live on Sharon's cooking, that's for sure. At least Virginia salts things, she says, and I am in a bind and too young to know what to say. Sharon's a good cook, says my father, and so is Virginia. (Am I? At nine?) You're too diplomatic, says gran, and my father says he's going to heat up some leftover green bean casserole. We eat a second dinner, the three of us, while mom finishes her evening routine and James retreats to his bedroom with a blunt and his phone. Anyway, says my father, finishing a thought he started ten minutes before: you don't have to be a good cook to be a good wife. I loved him for this offering, and in retrospect maybe kind words like these, made in my mother's absence, said more about their relationship than the hundreds of days I watched them be and not be together. He knew who he married, even if the rest of us weren't so sure. I think he wished he could be as aloof as she was, from us, from the whole world. Daniela, later, was another aspirational choice. He hoped the women he chose could make him more interesting than he felt. Maybe he succeeded. Maybe not. I learned to cook, eventually, because I loved completing things and then watching them disappear.

Tell me this, says Lex, when we are at the Pacific on a Saturday evening, sitting on the sand as the waves roll foaming and deep along the shoreline. Did you expect this, before? I ask: Us? Did I expect us? Yes, she says. I don't know, I say. I toss a piece of broken oyster shell away. My brain fell apart that last time we split. I got hard, I mean, against everyone for a while, not just you. I guess way back the first time around, I thought I could will us to forever, but that feels like a long time ago now.

She leans back and into the self-assured leisure of her body. Some people look like they might crumple into themselves when they relax, but she has always had the opposite posture: full, linear. She takes up more space when she is happy, and to be next to her is a lesson in vitality. It got to where you were the only person I wanted to impress, she says. Tough audience, I laugh, and she kisses me, and the air is hot. On the way home we listen to *Welcome Me* by the Indigo Girls and I roll down the windows and we're together forever right then. California can lie to you like that. It's good at fantasy.

The orange purple evening turned to darkness and she fell asleep in the passenger seat as I drove. When we got home, she stumbled in and crashed on the bed amidst our boxes, the fan humming on blast across her skin. I showered, taking my time. Black soap. Apricot scrub. Lemon Verbena shampoo. Her new gig started on Monday: Assistant Curator at LACMA. When she told me they'd offered it to her, I had joked it seemed a good metaphor for America's relationship with art, putting all those priceless sculptures and paintings directly above a tar pit. She said the tar pits were next door. I said: what does next door mean to a tar pit? She laughed, the way she always laughs, when I say something she is not expecting. I dried myself and crawled into bed beside her and we dreamed.

By Christmas I was getting antsy about what to do with myself. I kept wondering if I wouldn't rather hit up a day/evening gig on my feet instead of another slog at a desk. We frequent Cuties Coffee Bar on the weekends and discuss our future. The hibiscus tea becomes my stand-by. When she sees a posting for a volunteer gig at Best Friends Society, she sends it to me and says she'll pay the bills for a while. Suddenly my life is sunshine and dogs and kittens and I wonder how the fuck I(we)'d managed to do this. Money is still tight so we make our own fun. On Friday evenings, we drive to unknown neighborhoods and walk around, poking our heads into bars and peeking at the lit windows of other peoples' houses. She is ever the critic. What were they thinking with that door? she says, and I love the way the streetlights illuminate her body, angled and lithe in a way I will never be. I had not anticipated how time would slow as we got older, the great expanse of decades laid before us, unfilled and unknown. We stared at the future and practiced at fantasies of what we might become: what if we moved to Canada? I would suggest, or her rebuttal: what if we got a house in the hills? Death traps, I would say, and the conversation would turn to other possibilities: when you're running the Getty, when I'm poet laureate. Her options were always within the realm of the possible. I preferred the moon.

One dew-shine Saturday morning I crashed the car on the way to Ralph's (or someone crashed into me, whichever makes more sense). I was turning left and they were turning left and we met in the middle. My shoulder got tweaked a little and they claimed they needed three months of intensive physical therapy to recover. Insurance covered it all, thank god, but my days as a baby animal volunteer were over. She took a Lyft to meet me and we got Korean wings and beer and talked through how we would get a new car. I'd take full-time work and we'd both commit to saving at least $200 a month. Just a clunker is all we need, I said, and she agreed, though I could see the resignation in her eyes. It should have been easier for her to save extra money than me, but her job came with a host of social responsibilities. While the business lunches could be written off, less formal meetings with artists were more often not. The tabs added up. I pinched, with small eruptions of bargain shopping to soothe my sense of deprivation. The Goodwill on Beverly Blvd and Croft was my go-to. I figured the rich housewives of Beverly Hills were too lazy to donate farther from home; more often than not I was right. The secondary market was my day-to-day, but the car remained elusive. Five hundred saved and then we'd need a new air-conditioner. Two hundred more and it was time to finally tackle that pile of dry cleaning. Fifteen hundred in change and then we'd be desperate for a vacation. We should have abstained. We should have skimped more. No excuses, right? Especially with rent as high as it was. That's the American way—blame yourself, your lack of self-control, your indulgence, not the landlord, your employer, the government. The bus was my home. She took Lyfts and we fought.

Every after-work happy hour felt like an insult. Every kitchen accessory I bought on eBay made her roll her eyes. Where did you get that jacket? I asked, one morning, as innocently as I could, and she said she needed it for work. She said she couldn't go in looking like the artists she curated. I bought a new chest of drawers—the closets were overrun. We need a car, she said. You're telling me? I said. She said no more. Binge-watching ate our evenings and orders in ate our extra cash. The joy between us deteriorated. More Lyfts—I was running late, she'd excuse—and me, soothing my self-pity with vintage this and that while I settled into lesser pay at a permanent desk and an ever-ringing phone that was never for me. Hello, office of X---, so on and so forth.

Yvonne texted that I should meet up with her friend Janet who'd moved out there seven years before (you need more friends(!) she said), and the name conjured a shoulder-padded Amazon in neon colors from L.A. circa 1987, but I met her at the Normandie Club, and what showed up was a thoroughly modern, petite thirty-something from middle Long Island with working class, Italian parentage. The bar was dark like a good secret. I was fucked from the first hello.

She was a producer at Paramount—started as a PA she said—and when she asked me, I stumbled over my what-am-I-what-do-I-do. I landed on certainly no one compared to you, and she said thank goodness, I am so tired of networking. I laughed and lingered over her face with my eyes. She proposed a toast, to living on your own terms, and I responded: only on the best of days. Clink, sip, shift, smile. Yvonne has told me so much about you, she said. You write, don't you? Yes, I said, sometimes. Two terrible novels I would never show anyone if you paid me, I said. I admire that, she said. To know when not to show something. I feel like everyone publicizes the first thing that comes into their head these days.

Social media encourages it, I said. It does. I prefer Instagram, she said. It lets me travel from my bed. And where do you go? I asked. Other than my thirst follows? she said. Well, those too, I smiled. (We smiled too much.) Croatia, she said. Siberia. Wales. Buenos Aires. Chile. Western China. Ethiopia. What do you find? I asked. Silence, she said. I am always looking for silence.

Fuck fuck fuck fuck fuck fuck fuck fuck. I say nothing. The grass is greenest where you water it, I hear my father say in an echo chamber of my always-interjecting childhood. Sip, sip, clink, sip. I respond to her with Leroy's old line: I am always looking for a surprise. Do you find it very often? she asks. No, I say. Not often. We meet in the middle of our words, knees akimbo on too-high stools next to a warm wood bar. You're a surprise, she says. Oh? I say. Yvonne left out the part about your secretive eyes, she says. I blush. Did she leave out the part about my wife? I say. No, says Janet of the faraway Long Island. No, she didn't. I want to meet her, she says.

The bartender—he with sunbright hair and tanned skin around a late-braces mouth, asks, oblivious—can I get you ladies anything else? His vest is buttoned. His smile is not. Anything else? I repeat. Yes, she says. Gin and tonic for me, I say and she orders another old fashioned. I use the lull in the conversation as an opportunity to wind back to the restroom (retreat!). Friendship shouldn't be dangerous, I tell myself. No promises broken, right? No promises made. The restroom door opens, and a twenty-something girl walks out, dripping with fringe on a bodycon dress that shows more than it hides. I was never so flashy. In Portland it was more head-to-toe rain gear. Worn-out hoodies and Chucks. Maybe I was never even so young. I follow the white lines of the grout between tile as if they are a map to some safer destination—then pee, zip, return. The evening ends with exchanged emails and phone numbers and a promise to hang out soon. Yes, I'll text you, I say—but I promise myself I'll ghost.

Become a good memory, I say to her to myself, as I do laundry on Saturday at Lucy's while Lex gets her hair cut in Silverlake. She's shorn again, but instead of reminding me of our early years, I see her severity and self-indulgence. She asks me later what I'm thinking about, but I lie and say I don't know, nothing much. (Janet with no shoulder pads.) Do you think the wildfires will ever get close to downtown? she asks. Maybe, I say. I don't feel as safe here as I did when we first arrived, she says. Because of the fires? I ask. Yes, she says. Did you read about those white supremacists up in Portland? she asks. They've always been in Portland, I say. They've probably always been here too, she says. Sometimes I want to go back to New York, she says. They're in New York too, I say. True, she says, but I think I know how to avoid them there. She looks off, above the tops of buildings, and says: I feel so exposed out here, too much sky. Huh, I say, and here I wonder if I'll ever find enough—

When I am alone, on the bus, walking to the library, anywhere, I want to text Janet, want to get cute (or be cute?) to her (to someone—am I still cute to Lex? when was the last time we had sex?). But I don't. I don't! I am good—I adhere to a version of good I decide is respectful, because I am not technically violating our vows. Even Jimmy Carter admitted to lusting in his heart—but what about Rosalynn, oh Rosalynn, did you also? Did your eyes wander? I imagine her in the back yard in Plains, with the cicadas buzzing in the near trees. Rosalynn, did you ever consider walking away? Did you ever leave the yard, alone, just for a little while, to feel the wind on your cheeks, did you ever wish so badly to be yourself, only yourself, whole and singular, beneath God and sky?

Because maybe that is the thing, really: I want to feel in command of myself. To do something for me. Janet is my preoccupation, not ours. Mine. Mine to delight in, covet—her petite hands, bangs that fall just-so, and that wandering look that seems to search the future for direction between each quip. I want to linger with her in the in-between. My job is as trivial to me as the expectations of adulthood that once hung over my life. Finally, I text her and I am guilty, but alive.

She feigns shyness and then caves. We skip the veil of professionalism that is lunch in Los Angeles and meet for evening drinks, again—this time at BOA in West Hollywood, legs crossed beneath the naked, potted trees. What did you tell Lex, she asks me? and I lie to her differently than I lied to Lex. That I was going out, I say, although to Lex I said I was going to Counterpoint and a bar to read awhile, and I've got a copy of Zizek's *Violence* burning in my bag to make good on what I've said. She orders one of the house cocktails, and the waiter makes a drama of the smoke in the bottle when he arrives.

Theatre of the absurd, she toasts, and we clink our glasses and drink. I've fallen on old habits and it feels for a moment like we are in New York instead of Los Angeles and she is the mistake I should have made ten years ago. I watch her sip and then I watch the other patrons and the evening light betrays my fantasies, shining clear and buoyant as the smiles on every toned body that slips by. I know better than to be here, with her, but I will do what I want anyway.

We do not drink enough to get drunk, because tonight I do not feel like excuses or sloppy kissing. She tells me about work, and if I had been more interested in the gossip of Hollywood it might have been juicy—a complaint about Gary Oldman on set, an off-color wonderance at the longevity of Kirk Douglas, speculation about Colleen Camp's rolodex—but I do not care to linger there. Fuck the stars, I say. I want to know about you. I lean forward. I try.

I am the person that makes them look good, she says. And what about before that? I ask. Before that I was a kid who wrote bad poetry, she says. Your good taste stopped you? I ask. No, the movies. Becoming a PA and then so on ate my life. I've never been good at sticking with something because it was my idea to do it, anyway. Producing suits me. I like getting things done because someone else needs something, she says. What if I said I need something, I say. She smiles. And what is that, V? she asks.

It was a chance, but I flubbed it. I'll let you know, I said, my wit gone. Some veneer of satiety—or wavering desire?—was pussy-blocking my attempt at a goddamn affair. She kept going, changed the subject for me (thank god) and I drank for good luck. Jeff Koons is a real demon, she said, I just saw him in that *Price of Everything* movie and ughhhh. I think when I was a kid I always imagined the golem like him. From *Lord of the Rings*? I asked. No, from Jewish folklore, she said, my mom's Jewish—it's dad who's Italian. (I felt like an idiot.) There's something distinctly creepy about the way he talks.

I think Lex has met him, I said, and the mention of Lex reminded us of our illicit purposes. Janet leaned forward and over-enunciated, near my lips, jesting: you're lucky he didn't eat her bit by bit. I am, I said, or at least she is.

She leaned back and we sipped. I was bored. The whole conversation was reminding me how few people I actually found interesting. I decided to focus on the aesthetic of her. I drank deeper. The swimming high I sought hit me at the bottom of my second glass—she had said something, had been going on and on about the Mueller Report. What makes you squirm? she asked and I remembered how this could go. You, I said like a hail mary. I'd like that, she said, and so she made me, on her own dime, at the Beverly Hilton that very evening.

It was indulgent and irresponsible and selfish and I loved it. She kissed my sweating face and I batted her hands and after I wriggled beneath her, I took her myself, and loved her trembling wrist and the smooth and new bend of her stomach under my fingers. It was ridiculous that we had gotten a room when we could have just gone back to her place, but I wanted something extra and I could tell this was the first time she had broken any of her own rules. In round three I made her stand on all fours while I teased her ass with my tongue and finger fucked her spasming, open cunt. After she came, I let my hair down, let it scratch my own naked back as I straddled her face and she licked between my legs, licking, licking, while I held her head, tight and close, my own orgasm rising fast and sharp and too loud for the good company next door. When I left, I asked if she would be there in the morning, and I promised to return.

Lex said nothing when I came in. She'd left dishes in the sink and was playing some cowboy thing on her Playstation. Did you eat? she asked. Yeah, I said, and went to take a shower. She was still playing when I went to bed. After 1 a.m. she slid in beside me and whispered, there's no such thing as utopia. I rolled and spooned her. No, I said, there isn't, and I kissed the ridge of her shoulder blade. She got up before me in the morning and we did not stop and talk, really, for days, and by then the aura of my infidelity had already worn to an intangible. The next time Janet and I met, our kissing was perfunctory. We met up again and it was frantic. The rhythm of our speaking and touching rose and fell as we approached the asymptote of our identities—now rebel, next ashamed. It continued for months.

Missives from the east arrived in my mailbox. An envelope with a dried brown leaf inside. A letter with dripped wax on the pages. A picture of a deer skull amidst brush. It was Leroy. I wrote him in return, sent him songs I'd become obsessed with. He cast spells that hit me midstride to the subway; breathe, he whispered, I believed. I inhaled. It is not over, he sang. The clouds burned off the streets by noon. While my compatriots in the office stressed over the endlessness of emails, I was distracted by hunger. Lust energized my bones. What was Janet doing? I did not know. I wanted to know now. Before Thanksgiving I told Lex: I am going to Asheville for New Year's. It felt like a tradition I could handle. She said she was glad of it. Would do you good, she said, I can tell you're going crazy. I was.

Leroy is wrapped in a coat with a blanket on his knees, smoking on the porch when I pull up. The drive is so steep that I am nervous the emergency brake in my rental won't hold, but he assures me they haven't had an accident yet. Come in! he says, and I hug him, and I remember it is his face I return to, not the land. The fireplace is roaring, but they have no central heat. I put my suitcase next to the couch where I'll be sleeping. His sister's white pitbull, Peony, jumps and jumps at me for attention (he is dog-sitting). Shhhh, I say, and she sits. I've always known you were a witch, he says. I flop onto the couch and Peony flops down beside me. Are you still in love? I ask. You waste no time, he says. He is making tea for us and I pull a green and orange crocheted blanket off the back of the couch and tuck myself in for this first leg of the evening. He looks so much older than the last time I saw him, and I realize it is because of the new scruff-shadow of beard that frames his eyes and elongates his chin. Love, he says. Am I in love? IN love, surrounded, yes, it is ongoing. I am loving and loved. Will I get to meet him? I ask. Tomorrow, he says. He's at his mother's tonight—she needed help patching her roof before the next rain. He comes from less than we had, he says, and he doesn't need to say more.

We tell each other the story of our interiors and leave the details of our lives for later. The news has been a preoccupation, but we skirt from facts to fantasies—I have always wanted to go to Siberia, he says, and we imagine snow, and lives with different worries and concerns. People always say communism doesn't work, he says, but what about capitalism? he asks. Is this working? I'm sure both systems work for some and not for others, I say. It's who it works for that matters, he says, no one ever says that. He is not wrong. I love him his adamancy, his truth and anonymity among the eagerly performative. He does not have facebook or twitter. He reads. He talks to the man he loves, and when I visit, he talks to me.

The next day I do meet this love of his and he is tall and robust and his accent is hillbilly honey. Jeremiah, he says, but you can call me Jeremy. V, I say, although you can call me Virginia if you prefer. We have a lot of names between us, he says, and I say I suppose more than some, and he gets into it about yesterday and how they got the tarpaper down, but it's gonna be a couple more days before the shingling is done. Those asphalt shingles can be a real pain in the ass to pattern, he says, and then he looks at Leroy and asks what he's got planned for me. Thinking we'd go looking for some bent trees, he says, and Jeremy suggests a trail thirty minutes north. Cherokee bent them as guideposts, Jeremy says to me, and it is as though the Cherokee are all dead, even though we know they are not. Have you ever been out to Oklahoma? I ask, and he says he's never been west of Memphis, and I say the desert out there couldn't be more different than the mountains. Even the sky is different, I say, and he says no doubt, and we don't go further into it.

You seen this? he asks me, and pulls up his insta. Granny squares and queer bakeoffs, he says. Never thought I'd see it. What does your family think of Leroy? I ask, and he says that's not much of a story to tell. How do you like Los Angeles? he asks, and I let the subject change and say something general about the weather. We don't push the first encounter further. He offers his hand and says it was nice meeting me and leaves us to make himself a sandwich. Leroy takes a hit from his small glass pipe, then passes it to me. I inhale until I'm coughing, and then he tells me I oughtta get a jacket for the road anyway. Let's head out, he says, we'll see more of him later. I go to get my jacket and then wait by the door while Leroy kisses Jeremy goodbye and soon we are on the winding road, headed east and then north, with dead leaves frosted into wet-smushed piles along the road.

After a good twenty minutes, Leroy speaks. His father still calls him Jeremiah, he says, and won't admit me. Like to his house? I ask. That I exist, he says. How long has he been out? I ask. Since he was fifteen. He takes a sharp curb with one hand on the wheel and as the road straightens, he reaches for a pack of cigarettes and a lighter in the center console. He cracks the window and lights up. I oughta quit before I can't, he says, and I tell him I'd rather he was here when we're old. Do you think getting old is a curse or a gift? he asks, and I say, I don't know, both? Yes, he says, I imagine so. He turns off the main drive onto a gravel road that rises sharply with the elevation and then turns again, deeper into the woods.

I've been having an affair, I say. He nods. Takes a drag. Do you want to break up with Lex? he asks as he exhales. Not yet, I say. I'm not ready to give up on us again. Mm, he says, and he is newly inscrutable. Mm? I answer him: I am marking the time. Yes, he says, I know. We don't get into it right then and there, but I crave his approval in the silence. He drives on. The silence lasts ten years. I nod off with the to and fro of the road and then wake when he is parking.

In the winter air, goosebumps pop up on my bare neck and I bundle myself as tight as I can. He's wearing half as much, but that's his way. We find a trail into the canopy and the wind rustles the hardwood branches around us. A gray sky sits overhead and spring feels impossible. When at last we come up on a bent tree, I sit in the crook of it and Leroy searches in the underbrush for wild ginger and sassafras leaves. Not the season for it really, he says, but I like looking. He kicks the leaves around, knocking them away to reveal delicate plants beneath. I have heard it said that couples who are together for very long begin to mimic each other's facial expressions and it occurs to me that a body might also take on the language of trees and plants if left to their company for too long. After a while, he brings me a wristlet he's fashion of twisted vine and I slip it over the end of my sleeve.

We tread farther down the path, and I find a raccoon skull off to the side. I pick it up to keep. He turns and looks off to the right. I hear it too, I say, and we leave the trail to find the rushing water. It is larger than a stream, smaller than a river. A valley creek, cool and clear. He squats beside it and then dips his fingers in before splashing his face.

On the other side of the creek are a few crushed cans and empty beer bottles. We settle onto the ledge of a rock, pock-marked by water and time. I sit. He stands. We listen for animals, for how alone we are. We take in the leaf rot and pine sap smell, the lingering hint of hickory fire in the east.

He takes a deep breath. We got married, he says. What? I say. It was a just a Friday afternoon, nothing else new or special, he says. You keep the best secrets, I say. He looks down at me and smiles. Who are you having the affair with? he asks. I grab a pebble nearby and throw it blooping into the water. Janet, I say. She's petite and beautiful and bossy. Well naturally, he laughs. Do I really have such a type? I ask. You have proclivities, he says. Fair, I say.

The clouds have joined together over our heads and I look up for answers that are not there to be found. We're already boring, I say. Do you love her? he asks and I think for a minute that I do, but then realize I only feel like it's respectful to say so, and that is not enough reason to lie. No, I say. But I do want her to be happy. Does she love you? he asks. No, I say. And I think to myself that I wish she did, even though it isn't fair.

Leroy picks up a fallen leaf and tears it into ever smaller pieces. When Jeremy asked me to marry him he said he couldn't promise he really knew what forever meant, says Leroy. But he knew he didn't want to exist without a definite us anymore. I start crying and the tears fill up my sinuses as I attempt to hold them back, but I'm no good at it, and I turn red and snotty, staring at a gnarled oak(?) tree across the water. That's the thing about me and Lex, I say. I don't feel like we're an us anymore—we've turned into two thems.

Turn off your autopilot, he says, and I nod in agreement, but I don't know how.

11

Soap scum and some unidentified reddish haze cling to the bathtub walls (now three weeks unkept), and so I relent, and scrub. Rag, Comet, hand. I am on my knees, bent over the edge, rubbing and pressing the rag into the porcelain, hoping for a strange peace, as if my labor could calm my mind. At the MET, I saw sketches and paintings of women at their housework: laundry hung, floors being washed. Their hair inevitably tied back so as not to be a distraction. I am they. My uterus cramps like a capri sun in the hand of a first grader and I wonder if I'll be early to bleed. The blood finally does drop out of me and it soaks my underwear and I pause in the answer. Drink some water. Change my underwear and add a new thick Kotex between my legs. Listen for no one. Two midol down and I return again to my labor, avoiding other questions.

Lex doesn't do the bathroom; we've split the chores by preference. She doesn't mind dishes and trash take-out and vacuuming (if she has to choose), and I prefer this meditative shh-sh-sh-sh, sheet changing, and grocery buying. We drop off the laundry. It is our one luxury.

I am not supposed to enjoy this, and tbh, I do not enjoy it enough to do it often enough. I put her Dr. Bronner's and Irish Spring on the countertop so I can clean the tub nooks. In the hall the laundry is overdue for taking and the pile of it is a chronicle of our last week: Lex's left-behind blazers and ripped jeans, my black pants, button-downs, cardigans (rotated variations so as not to appear unkempt). Work is not bad, but it has offered little more than a steady boat. My coworkers are as amiable as I could ask for, but there is a distance between us. The obvious: that my solitude is chosen, not enforced. I make a strange newcomer, always preoccupied—

Here again the bleach and bubble smell intoxicates me. I open a window. We should get a cat, I think. We should not get a cat until I know if we are going to be together next year. We are married. Why would I assume we will not be together? I am not accustomed to the scale of permanence. Two days later she is getting ready for work and reminds me to grab some meat and veg or something for dinner on the way home. Jay is coming over, she says. Jay? I ask. She just joined the development team, she says. I told you about her last week—oh, I say, not remembering—but I do remember to get meat and veg (steak, broccoli, red potatoes) after work.

She cooks; I shower and change into a caftan because I feel dramatic. Jay shows up and she is a Lex facsimile through a scanner darling. They embrace. I shake her hand, warm, unsweaty, with fingers that feel like they can play piano. She removes her linen blazer, draping it casually over the back of a chair, and I wonder at why it never occurred to me to set a jacket over a chair top quite like that; it is clear that Lex has also observed and wondered at this woman's grace to the point of distraction.

We eat politely—we are all so adult, so practiced at good presentation—and then Jay and Lex linger at the table while I clear the dishes. Lex tries to help me but I shoo her away—who am I?—and they keep discussing Mueller. Every conversation circles back to Trump; we are in shock, trying to analyze the car accident in motion. I scrub the dishes and it feels silly to care, but I am glad I have something to do. The constant political incredulity wears on me, and the platitudes of supporters even more so. We are free, still—sort of—I have been told—but what of those who are not already? Won't be?

I bring them more wine and pour myself a glass that I drink alone, leaning against the kitchen cabinets and listening to the rhythm of their speaking. Each exclamation rocks to and fro, fore and aft. But then a turn—where did you grow up? I hear Lex ask. And Jay says she is from Southern Illinois. Flat as Kansas, she says. I've never been, says Lex. What's there? Weather, says Jay and laughs. Big sky, lotsa corn, a few towns, a few colleges. Chicago if you drive north at night, she says. Only at night? asks Lex. Only at night, says Jay, and she says it like it must be true, because it was true for her once, when she needed it.

I re-join them and sit next to Lex on the couch, but she leans forward, away from me and towards Jay, who is telling a story. Her mom was trimming her hair one night on the front porch as a thunderstorm moved in from the west. I settle back on the couch with my feet tucked under me. The air had begun blowing in these great gusts, she says, her hands waving, and the birds were so quiet. Mom was standing in front of me and she'd tugged my bangs down over my eyes with a comb like this before she snipped and the wind brushed the falling coils into the grass. Our dog Boomer was barking on the stairs, like she could scare the storm away. And you know even though, technically, I know how the sky holds so much water, it always feels insane when that kind of rain happens, like the ocean has flipped upside down. Mom only ever let me run in the rain if there was no lightning. Otherwise we had to go inside, sometimes to the basement. Have you ever heard a tornado siren? she asks. We have not. They're like how I imagine air-raid sirens probably sounded during World War Two? Fucking loud and terrifying.

I've always been afraid of storms, says Lex. In New York we'd get good nor'easters and sometimes a hurricane, but nothing like your tornados and barn crushers. They're wonderful, I say, but maybe I only think that because I grew up without them, and then I realize this is the first thing I've said in over an hour. I guess they do have their own kind of beauty, says Jay, and it is hard to believe she isn't everyone's lover.

We say nothing about her when she leaves and I know within a few weeks that Jay and Lex have been seeing each other, as I have been seeing Janet. Stolen kisses in cars. Memes sent like inside jokes over text messages. We do not talk about it. I assume that Lex knows where I am when I am out, and I assume that Lex knows that I know she is out with Jay. We stop caring so much about how clean the bathroom is, whether the clothes have been done. She takes up the brush. I secret myself in coffee shops, alone, writing like I haven't—really—ever. When we do see each other, it is at night, surprised in the kitchen. I was feeling peckish, she says, standing naked with an apple in her hand and the refrigerator door open. I want some ice cream, I say, and she moves aside for me in my grandma gown. I open the freezer door, she leans close behind me and smells my hair. It's been a while, I say, yes, yes, she says. She turns me around and I hold her head in my hands and stare at her with every held-back word. I kiss her and she pulls my gown over my head. We drop to the floor and claw at each other like fighting dogs. She throws the apple, I rise above her and hold her down with one hand on her shoulder. She grabs me and we are kissing and I finger fuck her to coming. Her back bends away from the floor and I run my tongue down the length of her body, then up again to kiss her beautiful cunt. I get up. She looks at me like she doesn't know me. I go to bed and she follows and we sleep in tandem—uneasy, two new-old lovers at rest.

Friday next, Lex goes out with Jay—probably up to the Observatory, somewhere public/private with dark corners to kiss in—and I stay home. Living room, tidied. Kitchen, cleaned. I wrap myself in blankets and make myself tea. Watch old episodes of *Unsolved Mysteries* on Amazon Prime and roll the sounds of America's regional accents around in my head, tumbling them with my own memories, staring again in the grass, looking for the other experiences of the past that I now know only as feeling. My grandmother's crocheted blankets—hideous with sparkle yarn in inexplicable places. My mother's housecoats. My father's pens, left around the house. Set pieces in a room where uncertainty lived, and smallness. My body, too, so tiny, with table tops flat above my eye line. Voices down the hall. Bare feet. Hunger. Go outside and play. Play in the grass where the head had fallen. Steal some candy from the corner store. On the television the husband says they never fought and I know he did it. Update: he did. Dad would never have said that. Never said much either way. He kept their marriage to himself, until she left, and then he said too much sometimes, what I didn't want to hear: don't be like your mother. There is no magic place where you're free all the time and your stress goes away. I know, damn it, I know, I know.

Lex came in and showered and asked me how my day was and then we cuddled ourselves to sleep. She looked at me like she wanted to tell me something, but I did not give her the chance. This one was about a guy who ran away because he was clearly gay, I say, or today was fine—work was fine; it's not like our office is building bridges across great valleys. My job is a pantomime. I hold no hammer. I am an answering voice to another room. Can you get me [insert here]? Left word. They'll call back.

One weekend I finally get Lex to run off with me to the dead desert. We stay in a broke-down motel in Olancha and then rise at four in the morning to reach Death Valley before the sun has made it impossible to stand the heat. The layered sands and short scrubs ignore us. I see a lizard scurry into the shade of a rock at the interpretative center and we make it to the basin before nine. She steps first onto the salt-sand and I follow behind the ridged imprints of her boots. Other tourists—a few French and Germans, a Canadian or two—precede our crunching. The air above the ground is already beginning to wave with the heat. She makes it a hundred yards out and then turns around and puts her hand up to her forehead feigning faint, then laughs and extends her hand to me.

Slowly the normalcy returned to us. I broke it off with Janet after a drink in a hotel bar near Paramount Studios. Afterwards I bought a pack of cigarettes and smoked three in a row, then threw the rest of the pack away. Lex and I outlast our crushes; we give each other the gift of not explaining ourselves or confessing what is already understood. For this, I will always love her. She was more self-contained and solid than any person I have ever known. She made herself beyond reproach by living without lying. How rare that is.

We are all inside the house. Gere is still James, in his room, listening to ska. My smallness is a medium smallness, tall enough to be mistaken for a teenager, but I am midway to twenty, pre-teenage anxiety, pro-loitering. In a spiral-bound notebook I take notes on our family, on our neighbors, on my classmates. Not a diary; a collection of judgments. I am looking for something true. Trying to figure out how to say it when I see it. Tiffany is mean because she is afraid people will notice how boring she is, I write. Dad avoids us because he is afraid we will ask for something. Mom is unhappy but she smiles when she eats sour candy. Gran smells weird. I like Devon. I don't write a reason, and now I don't remember why. Later: Stephanie has a beautiful laugh.

Gere and I were siblings, but we were not accomplices. A separateness of age, gender—or was it sadness? I have said our family were a mixed lot; we may have been attached by blood, but we were differentiated by inclination. During my middle childhood his buddies would tear through the house back to his room in a whirl of noise, grabbing snacks from the refrigerator on their way. He was seventeen. They pretended they had important plans. Door closed, music on. I would go to the restroom and hear them. On an otherwise bland afternoon TJ opened my door while I was changing and stood staring at me half-dressed. Pretty little titties, he said, and then closed the door and went down the hall. I took to avoiding them as much as I could. I didn't tell anyone because I didn't want to answer questions that felt like accusations. In secret I hated them all—not with a mixed hate like I knew movies wanted to believe pre-teen girls harbored for older guys. No, mine was real. Specific. The kind that could have burned whole towns in white fire if I just had the breath I dreamed. Not a molecule in my body envied their sloppy violence. I detested them and held their brute adolescence in contempt. And I loved that I knew I could hate like that.

Gere had a girlfriend. And then another. They had names. I've forgotten them. I knew he jerked off all the time because his laundry had a self-renewing pile of hand towels sloppily tossed in with his pants. My dalliances and masturbation were more covert—in the bath, door locked—so clean, so clean. No leftovers, only quaking. Maybe someone noticed I was suddenly exhibiting a love of baths. More likely no one noticed at all.

The truce of our family was kept tight by our secrets. We presented what we wanted to present, when we wanted, and revealed only what little needed to be shared to stay a unit. Our atomization freaked out my babysitters but was hardly considered a flaw amongst ourselves. Was it Jen? I called her that before. Jen didn't last. I thought maybe when she heard about me staring at the head from the wreck she figured I was too much of a weirdo to spend time with, but her little brother accidentally told me differently, years later in high school. Said my family was full of nymphos. Said she'd walked in on my mom with her hands down her pants in the pantry, having phone sex with who knows who. I knew who: Brenda's Brent. Said if that wasn't enough my dad used to leave his jizz on the shower wall. Are you sure it wasn't soap scum? I asked. And he said all he knew was what she'd told him. We were parked out in Hood River, between a few dairy farms and the dark forest. Looking for meteors. His name was Robert? I think. Maybe he liked me. We spent a lot of time together for a few months of my sophomore year, then one afternoon he got caught in his neighborhood driving his parents' car without a license. He panicked when he saw lights, sped through a stop sign, and got booked. Juvie plus community service, then his parents shipped him off to one of those private bootcamps. After that I think they moved or something. We didn't see him in school again. And he didn't call anymore. Was disappeared. But before all that I told him Sasquatch was real, that I'd seen one when I was a kid when my dad was driving us home from Mt. Hood. Really? he asked. Really, I said, even though I was lying. He said wow, and then pointed out a shooting star.

I got up and kicked the dirt. We didn't kiss. I remember trying to get a look at him on the back of his truck from where I was standing, and he looked stuck, and young, and I wasn't much interested in either one of those things. From my notes: I am still a child. As a teenager I kept waiting to grow out of that feeling. Drank up beauty where I could find it, thinking a color here, a photograph there might balance the disillusionment. I couldn't hold onto my identity the way I heard other people talk about theirs. I listened for the habits of other cultures, wondered at what it must feel like to inhabit their expectations, even as I failed at living up to the standards of mine. I was on no track to be a good mother; and in this way, at least, I felt a kinship with Sharon. I could not forgive her the distance, but I could acknowledge her reasons.

Gere called while I was at work, left a message that he was stateside again. What're you doing in L.A.? I asked, after I got him on the phone, and I genuinely smiled. It surprised me to be excited to see him, and when he showed up in front of the office on Sunset, I gave him a hug like he was the prodigal returned. He wore jeans, no more orange drapes. Vivaan? I offered. Let's go with James, he said, and I said okay, and we walked up the Boulevard. The Viper Room was hot with loud music and so we kept going and let our feet set the rhythm for what we had to say. No one walks in L.A., he said, and I laughed and said it really was a shame, all us nobodies walking beside the traffic. He laughed and said it was good to see me. He told me he'd left the forest and spent the last eighteen months in Bangkok, teaching English. What were you doing before? I asked. Same-ole, same-ole, he said. Meditation retreats. Solitude. For some reason I thought you had moved to Thailand for love, I said. No, he said, I'm not very good at love. I slipped my arm through the crook of his elbow and we slowed with the gentle sloping of the sidewalk. Me either, I said, and he nudged me like he knew and was grateful.

We continued up to The Standard and he ordered a whisky ginger and I got a burger and fries. Outside, in the setting sun, a gray-blue haze clung to the ground. It was as close to cozy as Los Angeles offered, and we glanced at the cars passing through the foggy particulate in equal measure as we looked at each other. I miss mom, he said, after a few sips, and I didn't expect that. Me too, I said, I miss having her to hate. He drank; we drank.

She never wanted kids, he said. No, I don't think she did, I said. I think I used to want her to want me, or you, more than it ever seemed like she did. And I used to blame her for that—but now I guess I understand what it means to feel like everyone wants you to be something you can't quite be, or if not be, like they want something from you that you don't really have to give. Yeah, he said. Mom wasn't really cut out for wife life. No, I said. And you? he asked. I don't know, I said. I'm still trying to figure that out. That's a problem, he said. Isn't it? I asked and took a sip of his drink. He laughed. Let's get you one of those. He ordered another and the waiter brought it quickly.

It was warm and stinging. He handed me a CBD pen and I did not refuse. Do you think our lives have a shape? he asked and I took a drag and handed it back to him. Like a shape like a rectangle? I asked. Sure, he said. Maybe, I said. I think mine would be a bunch of scattered circles, he said. On the same plane? I asked. He thought a moment, and as he did, his eyes looked the same as how our father's eyes could reach into another room and pull back a memory. No, he said, I've spent most of my adult life trying to force them into the same plane, but now I think that might not be possible.

Then you are like mom, too, I said, and he laughed. I don't know it, but I bet you are too, he said. And what about dad? I asked. Dad is a line, he said and took a sip, I guess I used to fancy myself a line too, but now I think that was just youth. What even *is* youth? I said, and he quipped: it certainly isn't now. Youth certainly isn't now.

We had one more round and I managed not to tell him about Janet or the ocean of reasons for why I wasn't so sure about wifing. Instead we played remember when? until the sun had set and the boulevard was alight with pink and gold. Where are you staying? I asked. And he said he'd gotten a room at a motel down on Olympic. That's near us, I said, good, I said, and I got us a Lyft and hugged his neck and promised to see him in a few days.

I didn't get the chance. He emailed and then took off for Colorado again, one of the few states left where the perpetually seeking believe they can still hit ground. A few months later we talked on facetime and he seemed happy. I think I expected to hear that he was dead, not because of some unspoken darkness, but out of his frequent desire to resolve. Instead he threw himself into mundanity, got a job as a waiter again, and on a snowy day, fell in love. She's a burn nurse, he said, and it suited him to meet her during night hours in the hospital parking lot after his shift was done at the Italian place (Nonni's?). I'm gonna take a few hospitality courses, he said, and he followed through. He grew tomatoes and taught himself how to sew curtains for his place. He stopped trying to answer every question.

I didn't see him again until after the wedding, while they were winding their way up the PCH, astonished at the changing land beside the sea.

Lex couldn't make it for lunch and so the three of us sat on a balcony alcove eating salads and chatting like I never imagined could happen with my own brother.

Diedre makes these extraordinary quilts, you wouldn't believe, he said, and pulled out his phone to show me pictures. I'm just so glad I finally get to meet you, I said to her, and she said your brother acts like he's never seen a blanket before, and she laughed the laugh of someone who didn't need to disappear to find themselves. Her voice had no money in it, no pretension. Are you from Colorado? I asked. She said no, Toronto. I thought I detected a slight accent, I said. Very exotic, she said, my Oooos. Charming at least, I said. James piped up like he was in a Dickens morality play: Diedre dear, have you met my sister? She's an interminable flirt.

I stuck my tongue out at him and then sipped my drink. We ordered a few greasy appetizers to supplement our salads and then sated ourselves with a banana split. It gave me hope to see the James that my brother had become, and in honor of it, I never called him Gere again. That evening, I came home and found Lex wrapped up in her winter robe even though it was summer, halfway through a pint of Häagen-Dazs. She hit pause on the movie she was watching and hollered at me while I undressed for the shower. Have fun? she asked. I kinda did, actually, I said. She meandered over to the bathroom and we talked through the shower curtain as I soaped and rinsed. And the wife? she asked. I pulled the curtain back and peeked at her. Canadian, I said. Grew up in Toronto. Charming.

Maybe he was just a late bloomer, she said. I shampooed. Do you think? I asked, because I didn't really want to speculate on it—at least not with generalizations like these. The truth was probably something harder to square, closer to what people have to do to find what they're willing to live with, but our conversations tended towards the rote and uninspired these days. Good day? Yes. Tired? Yes. Too much like the help desk at a hospital. I got out of the shower and she switched over to some new comedy series. Never seen it, I said. Jay said it was alright, she said, and we watched. I was indifferent to the mention and I realize, in retrospect, that my indifference should have been significant, but what do we know of ourselves as life is unfolding? We weren't ready to part, and so we did not imagine ourselves parting.

The show is better than we expect, and for a few hours we forget that we are bored with each other. We laugh and townie life looks suddenly appealing. A night passes. Then a few weeks. We sail through the seasons. And then we wait for more.

12

My life was very white in Los Angeles, despite living in Koreatown, despite roaming the city's many neighborhoods—south and east. I did not know how to enter into established networks of friends as anything but a tourist. TBH, I didn't have friends anymore, at all, really. My world shrank from its expansive throbbing in New York and that old never-know-what-will-happen luster became a quiet hello. A different life, of a sudden. More time to think. As when I was a child, I read. Slouched in my bed, open books leaned against my knees. *Middlemarch*, *Down Girl*, *Empty Without You*. The pages sliced through hours and I marveled at my revived peace of my mind. Lex had begun her own deep concentrations. She taught herself Final Cut Pro and spent weeks splicing footage and sound effects and credits together into mini-tours and teasers of the LACMA exhibits. I thought we should start supplementing the curriculum guides, she said, of her third video in a month. Her face became a front-lit hovering dream, lights out, with only the screen to reveal her. I secreted myself with my books in the bath, wrinkling pages with my fingers, and dove further and further into irrelevant anonymity. It felt safe, to be hidden, to close the door and turn away.

When we had enough saved, finally, to buy a car, we got two. She wanted to lease; I thought it was a waste of money. She went to a car lot; I went to Craigslist again. She drove a MiniCooper. I drove a Corolla. When I rode with her, I prayed we wouldn't get crushed, and I marveled at the leather details of the interior and how the smallness of each dial magnified the largeness of her. I knew she had not gotten taller or gained weight, but it was clear that she was coming into herself. I could look at her face and see the middle-aged woman she would be, like the women I saw as a child in grocery stores, gently squeezing wedges of brie before placing them into their shopping carts. Women who wore long scarves and had wrists that could write symphonies. For a few years in my teens, I had believed that I would grow up to be such a woman, but now that I was older, I knew that I would never have that kind of grace. Finesse was not in my repertoire. I suppose it was my testy, inherent suspicion of hierarchy that kept me from cultivating top-drawer habits and truly Mame-like grandiloquence. Regardless, she had succeeded, and I resented her success in it.

She wore her hustle the same as Marilyn wore her femme drag. Breathy attention, exclamations of interest—false, false—and still so captivating. The rich want to believe in the hologram. They always want to believe. Lex offered a wide-eyed smile as she shook their hands, a look practiced in our mirror, caught while I glance up from *America Day by Day*. You look ready, I say. She says she's so tired of it, that she wishes she could stay home with me, but I don't believe her. I smell the perfume on her shaved nape, and the lip balm on the edges of her lips. She is ready to eat them alive.

Can the hologram grow flesh? I wonder, after she leaves. And then more terrifying: how am I so sure which is the hologram?

It was my fault I hadn't been to East Texas to see dad and Daniela since they'd moved their brood south. I was better at saying next year than saving up the money to visit them. Erroneously, I had convinced myself that Oregon must be so much more amenable than Texas, not because of climate but people. The truth was that in both places the people were pretty much the same with only minor differences—diet, chief among them. Not many peppers in Oregon cuisine. Four-wheeling, work, Jesus, and a gnawing suspicion of anyone who wasn't "like them" (read: white) were in common. For my father, the piney woods had plenty of wood to cut and hew. He sat in an office that smelled like paper glue and sawdust and signed invoices and answered calls and wrote memos about bulk orders from wood flooring concerns and construction outfits, the same as he had before. I had reconciled myself to the visit, but I still wasn't exactly happy to be there. This part of Texas lacked the mediating sanctuary of Rothko or the lilting guitar tunes of country-western hopefuls. We were close enough to Lake Charles to smell the smoke on westerly winds and hidden enough in the pines to feel like the earth was small and young and without variation. Belts and saws warbled and seared in the sawmill. Rough-knuckled men nodded their heads at me as I passed their dusty faces. Boss's daughter. My father, the middle boss.

How's Lufkin treating you? he asked as he gave me a big hug and then gestured at the loveseat across from his desk. I sat. It's interesting, I said. The room was small, and the mumble of the machinery outside hummed behind every word. Daniela told me you said it'd be fine to come up here. Didn't really feel like helping her with Ryan and Marialese, I said. You've never had much of a reputation for doing what you don't feel like, he said. I'll stay out of your way, I said. It's good to see you, he said. It is, I rejoined, and it occurred to me that he thought of us as similar.

The rest of the afternoon I putzed around on my phone, facebook-stalking old lovers and liking posts by my NY friends. NY was another lifetime ago and the sights and smells of where I currently waited hovered around me in strange and unfamiliar closeness. Dad looked as at home as he ever was in our house when I was growing up. Calls in, calls out. His accent had changed into a tighter enunciation. Shipping out to Nacogdoches, he said, and the NACK popped out of his mouth the opposite of the KIN he swallowed when he said Lufkin. I wandered to the restroom. Sat too long on the pot scrolling on my phone, watching kitten videos. Bounced up and back to dad's office when I heard someone else finally come in. The afternoon dragged slower and slower, and it felt like this was my life now. When I had become newly reacquainted with that kid quality of boredom, he finally said closing time, and we left.

These days he drove a big family-size SUV, complete with seat holders for iPads. Discarded toys and random kids shoes littered the floorboards. I buckled myself in, took in the sight of him in this setting, and the reality of his continued (or disjointed?) fatherhood undercut my sense of belonging. My dad was someone else's dad. That's what time had done.

At the house, Daniela did her best not to resent me. I didn't blame her. No doubt my presence was a solid reminder of what in my father she would never relate to. In this house I was the leftovers forgotten in the back of the fridge, a bit moldy, but still there. She wasn't working right now because in real money it cost less for her to stay home than for them to pay for childcare. She put on a good smile, but she wore her dayboredom heavy around the eyes. Back in Portland she had been a brand coordinator at a big ad agency. Texas STAHM had not been in her plan, and I wished then that I had a better bridge between us than this awkward step-whatever to discuss her disappointment. Want any help setting the table? I asked, and she mouthed thank you over the heads of the twins, already seated with crayons and construction paper spread out like a multicar pile up across the table. I got the plates and set them at the end before telling the kids it was time to finish up. Gotta make room for supper, I said, and Ryan said why? like the brat he was. Because you have to eat so you don't turn into a bridge troll, I said, and he said he wanted to be a troll, and then Daniela intervened. Listen to your tia, she said, and I didn't mind it. We both knew that step-sister felt weird to us both. Tia me.

Marialese, who was less clumsy and crueler than her brother, gathered the paper from the table and laid it in a stack on the kitchen countertop, with her own drawing on top and his in a small puddle left by the dishrag. He did not notice until after dinner, at which time he threw both their drawings in the trash. Marialese slapped him on the back. He kicked her in the shin. They were separated, and I retreated to the living room to distract myself with my phone again. But at supper, we all committed to the fantasy of togetherness. Even the kids stopped their feuding. Maybe it was the heaviness of the mac and cheese that settled us down, or maybe it was our collective, adult weariness.

My father ate in this house with a different commitment to etiquette. He kept one hand in his lap throughout the meal and spoke to his wife with his eyes as the kids unloaded their tattletales and wants. I had never seen him speak to my mother without speaking; theirs had been the simulacrum of a side-by-side partnership, while it lasted, with no face-to-face gaze. Watching, I was jealous of him and Daniela in their coupledom. That I was the offspring of a lesser love felt like I was wearing a hand-me-down shirt that already had holes in it. How much of me could be seen? Would I ever be warm?

They asked how my job was going. It goes, I said, as though I was talking about a train ride (which it felt like, most days, with people flitting from office to office, phone to phone like a thinning forest passing just out of reach). I sat, printed, filed, watched. It goes, I said, and my dad asked if I thought I'd stay there a while. I think I'll stay until I have a good reason not to, I said, which wasn't really the kind of answer he wanted. Lex seems to be doing well, he said, and I said yes, she'd been promoted, and he said she was a real keeper. Keep her, I heard, keep her, keep her, keep her. She's great, I said, and he told Daniela a secret with his eyes. Daniela spoke: how is L.A. compared with NY? she asked. I guess it is more spread out, less manic. There's an understanding that work shouldn't be all of life, but it's also hard to feel time passing, I said. No seasons. A woman should never be kept, I think, I do not say.

Los Angeles has such nice weather, says Daniela. I've always wanted to live there, she says. I didn't know that, I say. (She is being kept at home and she wants to be in L.A.) No doubt there are lots of job opportunities, there, for the kind of work you do, I say, and my dad interjects: not much lumber though. No, I say, but you won't work forever. Try me, he laughs, and it is the sound of my mother asking me to drink another glass of wine with her, just one more. The kids are pushing the food around on their plates and picking at the edges as though they are Breatharians. I never understood not wanting to eat, I say to Ryan, and he says I can eat his. He's full, he says. But he wants dessert. No dessert tonight, says Daniela. They are not pleased, and the small chaos ensues.

In the living room I listen and wait until I hear the family settle. Doors closed. I shower and tuck into the couch with my phone again. Text Lex: miss you. She says same-same. I like that she says it like that, like I would say. How's your dad, she asks, and I text back that he seems happy. And Daniela? she asks. Wasted, I say. Like on booze? she says. Nah, I say. Her life. The kids are alright, but there's more to her than this. Can't save'm all, says Lex. No, I say. There's a long pause between texts, and then I lie: gotta sleep. G'night bb, she says. I punch in my headphones, pull up an incognito window and watch some porn. Nothing's doing it for me. Put on Nellie McKay and look around.

They don't have many books, really. A few trade hardbacks. The living room bookshelves are full of family photos and decorative vases. Over the couch hangs a slab of whitewashed wood: *Live, Laugh, Love.* Gag a maggot. The berber carpet is hard, instead of soft. The blue couch I'm on, overstuffed and crowded with pillows, has at least some give. A big flatscreen tv sits blank over a hardly used gas log fireplace. A dark wood coffee table with no speakable design qualities. A recliner. A wooden crate full of toys in the corner. And on the far wall a sliding glass door leads to a Mexican tile patio and a back yard as barren as the Sahara. Everything looks like it was bought on sale at HomeGoods or on clearance at Ross. Almost distinct, but there are a hundred more on sale. As I try to fall asleep I hear, too loudly over the music, the nothing that is.

The next day I make an excuse to head out and take a Lyft to a coffee shop in town. It's populated by the usual ubiquitous crowd of creative hopefuls—in different genres, perhaps, than New York, but identifiably the same. Hop myself up on coffee—four cups—and spend the better part of the morning on Metafilter and the early afternoon half-watching Carrington in a window in the corner of my desktop while I online shop for jeans I can't afford. When it seems bearable to return to the house, I head back without warning and no one is home. I walk around to the back yard and sit on the covered patio and wait. Hook up to their wifi and mess around on the computer some more, then close it. Feel the heat, watch the ants. A crow comes and hops around near me a while, then leaves for something better. The sunbleached grass is crunchy where in other climates a green softness might live. A lizard slinks around the house and climbs the wall under the back window. I watch it run and pause, run and pause. Get nervous. Pull out my phone and scroll through Instagram.

Some Hollywood stills, a cheap old house for sale in Wisconsin, Cecilia posting her breakfast in New York, and then I see that Lex has posted a mirror selfie in a bathroom as tagged with graffiti as Mars Bar used to be, now chopped up and bought by some richo hoarding the artifacts of poorer people's culture like it could make him cool. She's darker in the lowlight, and I can see her mother's worry behind her eyes, but her gaze is a reckoning. She isn't smiling. Her chin is up. Whatchu got or you don't know me or wut. Thoughts imagined. I double tap.

I used to be so much better at sitting. On other afternoons, as a child, I would stare at the grass, watching its slow movement and the safari of small insects and slithering creatures that made their home where we rarely look. Hours lost to observation, and I did not expect or want entertainment. It was enough then to be outside in the quiet, alone. But latent anxiety has replaced contentment. Shouldn't I be posting something to Twitter? Shouldn't I be uploading pics to Instagram? Undocumented moments slip unnoticed, coveted but soon forgotten. The lizard was green, that ran across the wall. The wall was beige. I feel guilty that I didn't get a picture.

The kids tumble out of the SUV screaming and wake me up from the head-slumped nap I've been taking. I rub the crick in my neck and walk around to the front of the house as Daniela sets down four grocery bags to get her keys out of her purse. I grab another load from the car. There are too many brightly colored yogurt drinks and mushy fruit sacks for comfort, and so I offer to cook dinner as we're putting everything away. Daniela seems astonished by the idea, but she doesn't protest. My kitchen is yours! she says, and I take the opportunity to spoil her a little. When she collapses on the couch and Ryan and Marialese are fully distracted by the latest Pixar flick, I bring her a glass of white wine and return to my post. The flour and sugar and cornmeal aren't where I'd put them if I was organizing the kitchen, but I find what I'm looking for anyway. She kicks her sandals off and sips her wine, half watching the movie, half watching me. Based on the ingredients I'm finding I decide on baked chicken thighs with couscous and sautéed zucchini. Side of freezer biscuits and butter. The chicken slips and slides in my fingers as I rub herbed butter under the skin. Did you cook much when you were growing up? I ask Daniela and she looks over at me, her wine glass held to the side, aloft, like a heretic's body of Christ.

My mother cooked for us, she says, and saunters over to me in her bare feet. Her hair is still pinned away from her face. Platanos and arroz con pollo, she says. Limonada de cocos in the summer. She used her spoon like a policeman's baton. And her avocado salad dressing was so good, she says, but I can't quite get the balance right between the lemon and mayonnaise, no matter how many times I try. I ask her when her mother moved to Miami and she says the seventies. Met my father at a night club, she says. I ask if they were dancing salsa and she says mostly cumbia. I don't know that one, I say, and she says she doesn't expect I would. There is no malice in her voice, but the weariness of invisibility and of holding a world in secret feels as though it might break the floor. My father was Cuban, she says, without prompting. My mother called him Toro Blanco. She laughs to herself and keeps her private memories. Did you like your parents? I ask. Yes, she says, I loved them very much.

I knew they had both died long before she met my father, but I also knew enough to know not to ask too much about that now. And you? she asks. I stop moving with the oven door partially open in my left hand and the heat rises over my body. I don't know—of course, I say, try to laugh it off (weirdly) flirtatiously, and then she says, is it of course though? I check the chicken and put in the biscuits. I used to hate my mother, I say, but I guess it was the kind of hate that has love in it. Dad—I have always loved—but to be honest, I've never really known what that meant. Or really, how? I don't know. Love was just assumed, I think.

Your father says you remind him, sometimes, of him, sometimes of her, she says.

I want to be drinking. I want to be able to choke dramatically—like in the movies—but I only eke out an oh! with gravel in my cheer. It was a compliment! she says. She says he said it after my mom died and she asked him what Sharon had been like when she was young. Michael said she was independent like you, that you remind him of the best parts of her, she says. I don't think I knew the best parts of her, I say. Daniela pauses and looks over at her Ryan and Marialese. It's hard to be yourself in front of your kids, she says, or at least the best.

Doesn't it bother you when he talks about her? I ask and start sautéing the zucchini. Nah, she says. How did you even meet my dad—I don't think I ever really asked. She laughs: No, you didn't want to have much to do with me in the beginning. I met him in the backroom at Huber's. She finishes off her wine:

I was between these two tall dudes? Like real tall, she starts. Later I found out they were Blazers players, and anyway, I ordered two tequila shots and a la paloma. The bartender had never heard of a la paloma so I started shouting him the recipe, and that's when your dad came over. I was getting ready to blow him off, but he opened the conversation by asking me what had kept me from my friends for so long and the fact is I wanted to talk about why I was late so I did. I told him about this pitch I'd been working on for a makeup company and just as I was about to go he told me he really enjoyed talking and would love to hear whether we got the account or not. Then he gave me his card. Never asked for mine. No guy had ever done that before, you know, just given me his number without asking for anything. It was smoooooth. I called him the next week.

It had never occurred to me that anyone in my family had a smidge of game. As if on cue, Dad comes in from work, announcing that something smells good. Daniela greets him with a hey there cowboy and a kiss, and I mumble "speak of the devil" and watch them with new eyes. Your lovely daughter cooked, she says, this woman who is a part of my family, his wife, and then she took her glass and plopped back on the living room couch from where I had first called her. I feel like I've missed something important, says dad, and he comes over to see what I was finishing.

I turn around and give him a big hug. You smell like wood like when I was a kid, I say, and he says he can't wait to eat whatever is cooking. I hand him potholders and a stack of trivets and he starts helping me get everything on the table. The kids say they aren't hungry because the movie isn't done, but Daniela prevails, and we sit down to eat as though a family, together.

Lex reminds me I am older now. Usually she reminds me of this fact by just being older, in front of me, this woman whose body has held years of my own lust in chaotic continuousness. But that Sunday she reminds me I am older now, and because of this fact, I need to go to the doctor. She's on the phone, calling from New York. I'm in my pjs on the couch and I haven't been to work in three days, done dishes in five. I'll be fine, I say. Jesus, V, she says, why martyr yourself? (This, before Covid. We didn't know how bad it could get.)

She's working on a big donation from an actress who makes up for her lack of skill by being a patron of painters and sculptors. She's become a favorite mark of the gallery set, but Lex has brought her a bag of In-N-Out all the way from Cali and knows the insecurities of the Hollywood successful better than her New York peers. They'll meet at a spa, no doubt. Lex'll get a pedicure beside her. She'll say it's funny how life works out, isn't it? and tell the story of how she started out painting and here she is, now, wining and dining like some bicoastal business maven. She's charming. She's good at this. The actress will be relieved that she has a sense of humor. They'll complain about the wildfires in California, the cold in New York. If only there was a place like Minetta Tavern on Sunset. Nothing will happen for two months. And when the actress gets back to L.A. she'll walk into LACMA one day and ask to see Lex. Lex'll take her to lunch, treat her like the Queen of England, and then the actress will donate enough to finish construction on a new wing. First exhibition: Women in Modernism.

Lex is right. I go to urgent care. They give me a steroid shot in my butt and it makes a sharp, sore bruise. Inhaler to help me breathe. Codeine to help me sleep (I sip it gingerly, save as much as I can for some other time). Antibiotics to kill the microscopic evil inside. In my fever I dream that Lex has a dick, but she won't let me see it. I get mad at her and make a grilled cheese sandwich and eat it alone. She comes in and kisses me and she's a woman again and I am so happy that I start crying, but then I'm alone in a padded room and my crying turns to sad crying and the ceiling becomes a gray sky. I wake up. She's still in New York and I cough and I cough again, because I feel like I can't breathe, and it is the codeine I reach for this time. A sip and it warms the throatline. Call into work the next morning, again.

That evening, I hear the front door open and wonder how long I can play dead before I start coughing again, just in case it's an intruder, but I hear the bags drop and know that Lex has come home early. Hey sicko, you still alive? she calls from the hallway. I sit up to speak, but cough instead. When she's in the doorway, I say I really am doing better than I was. I don't know if it's because she has short hair or because she is Lex, but she has the ability to look more unruffled after a six-hour flight than should be allowed. Her gray tshirt is hanging loose off her collarbone, French-tucked into her red John Varvatos jeans. The black sweater over both of them looks as New York City as the Empire State building and she's finished it off with black oxfords, a black belt. She's hot enough to make me feel guilty for ever wanting alone-time, but I cough again instead of saying so, and she comes and sits beside me on the bed. What happened to the comforter? she asks. I puked on it, I say. She plucks up the wadded tissues that surround me like (I want to think) a bed of crushed paper roses, but in actuality better resemble the trashpile I've been sleeping in.

She throws my effluvia into the garbage and makes me ginger tea. Drink up, she orders and disappears again to take a shower. It's spicy and steaming and burns my throat. She returns to our bed in baggy lounge pants and a tank. I can't believe you came back to nurse me, I say, and she laughs and says, you know it was a good excuse. She was bored. She puts her hand on my head and my body sinks into the bed, so tired and dumbly weak. You're on fire, she says. Not in a good way, I crack. She narrows her eyes with skepticism but still snuggles up to me. The fan over our bed spins round and round and if I stare at it too long it seems to stutter and reverse course. Being sick as an adult has none of the glamour and timeouts of childhood. As a kid sickness was an inconvenience. In this older body, illness is a threat. The veil is too close; mortality is as real as the dust on our bookshelves. She unrolls a blanket from the foot end of the bed up over top of me. I cough. Hang in there, she says.

I look for something specific—and maybe I have no right—but I want to see fear or an overwhelming affection in her eyes. I see only gold flecks amidst the brown, and the unfathomable gulf between our bodies, sick vs vital, tired vs alive. I was jealous of her, and fearful of our slow dissolving.

13

Ranging these western deserts on my weekends, windows down, I look for home. Watch jackrabbits hide in brush and Joshua trees raise their trunk arms to dark night sky. Mojave dirt and dust in the footwells and burrs stuck to my jeans. The Corolla gets me where I need to go. Time feels long and empty without movement; Lex is at openings and heading in early to micromanage the curators. I work and wander. In my solitude, I reach back for that early aching. She is a phantom to me, and when she is near, I feel I know her less than I ever did. The older I get, the less I can bring myself to assume or believe I understand anything about her, or anyone I have known.

I have what she has told me. What I have witnessed. But there is no getting inside that skin. I am never satisfied. Romances tell lies about fusion, as though any two people could melt into one being. But I see the air between our hands as we eat. I smell her body in our bed. I feel her absence when I am alone. She is apart. We are two; ever thus. The sun is hot and the night is cold. I carry water, peanut butter crackers, blankets. I eat tacos from street vendors set up on folding tables under tarps. She asks me what I find. Coyotes, I say, and rabbits. You still have the same luck, she says. As it was in the beginning, it is now and ever shall be—

We were all inside the house. Dad was taking a nap and James was playing video games in his room. My mother and I were in the living room, she sitting in front of the couch surrounded by recently developed pictures. White envelopes that they had come in were piled up with the negatives still inside. She flipped through the snapshots manically, sorting them according to criteria only she really understood. V, close your mouth when you stare, she said. It makes you look more intelligent. I clomped my jaw shut and sat on the floor next to her. You look so pretty in this one, I said, as I chose a shot of her in a fir tree forest near the coast, looking back at some unknown beyond and smiling. She picked it up and examined it. I was so cold that day, she said, and set it back down. Flip, toss, flip, drop, flip, set. She selected a picture album that she'd bought on clearance at the stationary store. Hand me those, she said, and pulled open the plastic fronting of the first page with a loud cluhkk-kk-kkk and then set a few pictures neatly on the adhesive before smoothing the plastic sheet back down. Nothing was chronological, but she was ordering the chaos. Here were the men of her life: her father, her husband, my brother, each caught off guard in the midst of play. Clyde, walking with a golf club in his hand, extended out in front of him as if he was moving to set it back inside its bag. Michael at a Beavers game, hands stretched upward in victory and glancing to the side, now caught forever, frozen in joy. And James, with his arms across his lap, bent over a Settlers of Catan board on a table between him and his friends. He stares upwards at the camera, annoyance in his eyes.

I realized most were pictures she had taken. Sweetheart, will you get me some water? she asked, and I went to the kitchen and brought back a full glass. She set it aside on the hearth as though she had forgotten why she wanted it. Don't sweetie, she said, when I accidentally knocked a few of her stacks askew, trying to sit beside her as small as I could make myself. She filled page after page with pictures of us and the places she had been. These weren't family albums—they were the closest record of her thoughts I would ever have access to, and I recognized the ethnographer's remove in each framed shot. She watched us; she preferred watching to knowing, and it hurt to recognize. I drank her water and she didn't notice. The pages filled quickly now that she had sorted us into the geographies she preferred. Gran and I were frequently placed together, and I resented the thought that we were in common. It was easier to be descended than grouped. The few pictures she had of herself she set aside until the end and then filled the beginning of a mostly empty book with them. Flashcards of her emotions. She paused and flipped through them as if she were learning about a stranger, so strange, my mother, my mom.

When she was done she asked me to grab a couple binders and we took them to a bookshelf where she had cleared a space in the hall. Now if only I can keep them current, she said, and I didn't understand what that meant. You're such a good photographer, I said to her, and she bent down to my level so that we were face to face and smiled. Maybe you'll take pictures someday, too, she said, and I was overwhelmed by the attention, rare and precious and terrifying. James came out of his room and wandered down the hall, and she immediately popped up to make way for him, then left to lie down with dad, or do whatever she did when we weren't watching. I went to my room and closed the door and wondered what it would be like to be an adult, and I hoped my life could be interesting enough to have secrets.

—world without end, amen, amen. The bitterness I have seen on other women's faces, dropped over their eyes like an immovable veil, haunts me still. I am afraid of becoming like them. Too many years, overly tired. Loftiness was never the goal, but this sameyness, spinning out the weeks and months in Los Angeles, is driving me mad. At least in New York I knew when I was older because I ached, and the air had grown cold and uninhabitable. These LA respites of rain in December and February and June are not enough. While Lex is working late, I read Wikipedia entries of notorious murderers, starting with the Manson family. Something twinges in me—a recognition(?) at their wide-eyed hunger, sanity lost, belonging found. Too much of this city is taken up by fools looking for their audience, with barely an identity between them. They're flesh bags of reaction. Dolls as easily animated by cults as directors. Why don't we call people serial murderers? I wonder—always serial killers. Serial episodes. Serial numbers. Serial days.

A promotion is on the horizon and Lex expects a title that will match her hard-won power. After a particularly stressful week, I wake up on Saturday to her throwing out her paint-splattered tshirts and heavy work aprons. She makes a pile of her unused canvases on the sidewalk and then she sees me, aghast, watching her in my pajamas from the window. She comes back in: I love art, but it's foolish to think I'm still an artist, she says. There are knives in her mouth. She goes straight to the closet and I watch, without speaking, as she drags shoes and clothes and formerly precious but seldom used handbags and towels and paint and paint brushes and cassette tapes and cds and board games and more crap from inside.

Do you want these? she asks as she holds up some torn button-down smocks. Yes, I say, and clutch them away from her. What about these? she asks about a stack of different colored chinos. Sure, I say, I can cut them off into shorts. She moves like a metal toy, bending to sort them, up again to turn towards the closet, reaching for what's next. The motion repeats itself. Her eyes squint, and periodically she pauses to ask me if I want something else. I wish I could keep it all, but I have no interest in magnifying the differences between us. She is unburdened and I am covetous. I say no and point at a camouflage jacket she's tossed aside.

That jacket looks so good on you, I say. It reminds me of holding hands in New York, I say. It doesn't feel like me anymore, she says and sips a glass of water, surveying the stacks. There are teeth marks on my arm. The piles are too similar to the chaos of what she left in Astoria, too full of what we have collected together. That was dissolution, then. And now? What is now?

I take a shower to distract myself. I obsess over the ways I've aged and not aged in my nakedness, softer in my belly but in the same general shape, with a creeping darkness under my eyes. We have a good life, don't we? This mutual togetherness. We have survived ourselves, even our own affairs. When I get out I dress and say I'm gonna grab a few things at Ralph's and she says she doesn't want anything and that is the essential difference between us, at least that's what feels true when I am alone, roaming the aisles, buying candy and milk and cucumbers and pasta, alone.

When Obama won the election in 2008, Portlanders left Obama/Biden signs in their yards for months afterwards as if the very hint of their support could inoculate their liberality from charges of racism. The months before Leroy left town were spent on my bike, riding in the rain and holing up in bars, alone, with him, and with other friends, sipping beer and filling the hours. In big groups I stuck to safe pantomimed opinions and debates over the merits of *The Big Lebowski* and the oeuvre of Prince. I felt strongly about neither, but there is a certain person my age who enjoys playing hockey on familiar ice. Leroy and I discussed cadavers, the rate of cell decay, the beginning of *Giovanni's Room*, the genius and limitations of Fellini, whether we would live to see the end of man, what people might evolve into if enough of them survived the catastrophes of climate change, where we might travel to, someday, if we ever became rich enough to do it, Gus Van Sant's childish worldview, the transcendence of Gene Krupa's drumming, how creepy the dude protagonist is in *The Gang's All Here*, what has been lost and gained with the digitization of film, who we imagined ourselves becoming—if we did, when we did, what we were avoiding the most. I got hungry, wanted Chinese. We ended up at Hung Far Low and huddled together in a dark booth, watching each other's eyes flash over the flickering light of a red candle. Kung Pao chicken for me, General Tso's chicken for him. Bad cocktails. And we would find other spots on other nights, until he was gone, because he had to go, and I was left behind to assess what life was possible in that place of stagnant goals and bleak new developments.

My last months in Portland crept by, filled by weekend roller-skating at Oak Park and long walks by the Willamette, beneath the bridges, stopping to watch the boats pass on their way north or south. When I skated I lost my future, forgot my past, slipped into a crisscrossed and spread-legged rolling wonderland, thighs burning with each passing minute. Skating backwards was as expedient as gliding forwards. Spinning as rational as a good sit. I returned again and again to feel the week disappear, barely real compared with the vibration of plastic wheels on the shellacked and polished wood. Outside the rain broke into long sunny days and waving greenery. I knew it was beautiful, but it was lonely, and I wished, like in college, that I had lived my life already. Too many questions. Too many uncertainties. Was I wasting time? Should I be trying to be something? Guys older than me with master's degrees were manning the checkout at New Seasons. Bartender was a thing people I knew were settling into. Others went back to school for another degree. Odd jobs on craigslist. Typing transcription services. Advertising (ughhhhhhhhhhhhhhhhhh)—they were the proudest. I picked up a gig in the burbs, making coffee, updating spreadsheets, answering the phone. Then another. Ate ramen every night. Eggs on toast for breakfast. Bagged salad lunches with lime juice and salt and pepper—avocado if I was splurging. I saved $7K, kept it quiet, then I left for NY. The American journey is supposed to be west, but if you start in the west, you go towards the sunrise.

It occurred to me that I was the villain. Lex knew I had gone for a drive but she didn't know where to or for how long. When I jumped on the 10, I wasn't so sure about either myself. She was in the office on Saturday again. I was at home putting away the dishes and looping on my own loneliness. I was so unhappy—unhappy with suffocation, unhappiness like a locked door and no key, unhappiness with secret friends: rage, frustration, my mother. I threw one of the plates in my hand into the sink. Threw it hard to shatter and it broke into sharp blue and white patterned edges. The pieces looked like they could become something else with enough intention, a better idea, some glue. I didn't clean it up. I left with my hair wet, with no extra clothes. I took my wallet, my phone, my keys. I turned off all the lights and drove.

We were all inside the house. James was bigger than me, like he always was, and mom had put on a dressier dress. Dad was sitting in the living room, reading the paper and waiting for us to finish getting ready. It was Easter and gran had decided we should all go to church. I didn't know Jesus from anyone's housecat and gran didn't approve of my mother and father's laissez faire and near-nonexistent spirituality. You're raising these children without rituals, she said to my father as the holiday approached, and so he had spoken with my mother, and they had relented to her influence. We would become the sort of family who appeared in churches at random, whenever gran couldn't take it anymore, and then we would disappear, back into the domestic squalor of our heathenhood.

I liked the part about getting a new dress. Mine was store-bought and made of blue linen. We look our best to honor the resurrection, said my grandmother as she put a bow in the ponytail I'd made. What's a resurrection? I asked and she said it was THE resurrection of the Son of God and I asked if that was Jesus and she said she was glad I paid attention sometimes. I still didn't know what a resurrection was, but it sounded important and when we got to church, I found out it was the sort of thing that made people happy. The walls were decorated with drapey white fabric and this church had a trombone and a French horn and trumpets for their Easter day. It's not always like this, said gran to me, but because it was my first impression, it felt like it maybe was always like this, here, forever.

My mother insisted on sitting next to me and so we filled up a pew: gran, me, mom, dad, James. James found a book that we were supposed to write our names in if we were visitors, but dad told him to put it away, and so we sat in the congregation unaccounted for. The pastor welcomed everyone and then the choir sang "Christ the Lord is Risen Today!" and the room vibrated with their joyful noise. We warbled through it, and mom knocked the side of me to cut it out when I kicked the pew in front of us. I can't say church was fun, but it got into me, and existed in the background of my head alongside every museum visit, every hike in a national park.

The holiday pattern began with the Methodists, but was followed quickly by visits to the Catholics and Baptists, Presbyterians and Four Square, Episcopalians and non-denominationals. We found high church with formal-ish dresses and suits and carpeted sanctuaries and we found contemporary church with jeans and khakis in repurposed strip malls and gymnasiums. The music was beautiful and unfamiliar and the words—pulpit, grace, benediction, benevolence, beatitudes, redeeming—were a door into wondrous confusion. Some congregations gave an impression of desperation; others an imperious reserve. I preferred the Methodists, and we returned several times, but never enough to belong to any one church, let alone any one tradition. Mom never believed, but my father courted a distant faith of muttered prayers and expectant blessings. James got curious about eastern traditions and quickly treated our sporadic attendance as a chore. I observed and wondered at the other families. Who really believed? Who could ever say?

It wasn't until I was older that I understood how the cosmology of it had booted up inside me. The possibility of an omnipotent anything was miraculous and terrifying. In physics, when I learned that time itself was a whole dimension, as real as this world of space and matter, I could not grasp the shape of it. I wanted to be able to visualize how time passed (or did not pass, but was), what its edges looked like, but I could not get outside of each passing minute. I decided that's what divinity must be—knowledge of space outside of time—and I left it at that, without personhood or power or name.

Los Angeles faded away. I went out looking for nowhere at first, and then I headed towards the false dayglow of Vegas, shining behind the shadowed mountains. I needed a place that felt alien and I trusted the zombieherd of resigned gamblers and wasted money, electricity, and forgotten reasons because it was fucked up and honest and I couldn't abide pretending like there was anywhere in America that didn't worship money, that wasn't complicit in everything that ailed me. The city did not disappoint. I rolled into an all-you-can-eat crab legs buffet a little after sundown and I cracked and sucked and watched and deflected until my stomach hurt and it made sense to get a room and watch the good and steady noise of pseudo-scifi tripe on the History Channel. Television has always bored me, but it could do sometimes as a friend substitute, a fact not lost on Warhol and other lonely hearts of other lonely rooms.

Outside my room, the hotel creaked and groaned with the hall noise of drunken stumbling and exclamations. When I ventured to get ice, an over-the-hill Texas bro got into his version of friendly, opening with a complaint about the drive and ending with a toast-adjacent raise of his plastic beer cup. Was supposed to snow in the mountains, he said, but you know these weather guys. They can't predict tomorrow and yet they expect us to believe they can predict global warming!

Huh, I cowed, and retreated with my ice bucket to my room. Where you from? he yelled at me, when I was already down the hall. Los Angeles! I said and disappeared. Deadbolt, locked. Ice water beside the tub. I slipped into the bath and couldn't stand the heat. Turned on the cold water and sucked at the ice. Isolation, as large as my certain heartache.

I'm going for a drive, I had texted, already two hours away. I knew I'd given the impression I was only going out for a little while.

The water vacillates between too hot and tepid as I add cold then hot water again, wait, feel faint, then add more cold. I have never been good at baths. The ice I draw in swipes across my collarbone, leaving traces of frigid water like glistening snail trails on my skin. Time passes. No measure except my breath. I drain the tub and start over, on my back with my legs spread beneath the faucet. It has been a while. I imagine bindings around me, as though Lex has lowered me into a vat of water, but the thought does not excite me like it sometimes does. I scroll through fantasies of high seas trysts and torture by Catwoman and then snap into a memory: Lex's close breathing beside my ear, both of us in the back stall at the bar she tended when we first met. The water has risen around me and I am rocking, subtly, with its buoyance. She pressed her bound breasts against the front of me while I sucked the air from the room, first in small pants and then in slow and measured exhales. Our breath evened into the same metronymic beating and then she kissed me. I grabbed her shirt by the collar and tugged her closer. She undid my pants with one hand and pulled my head closer to her face with the other. I feel my nipples crown above the water and then I bend, slightly, towards my center and they fall again below. I arch, they emerge. The torrent of water on my clit becomes a crushing pulse as I move into and away from its constancy. She ran her hands through my pubic hair and then rubbed the top of my clit with her flat fingers, slow and faster, slipped so carefully into my underwear. When I came, she shoved the side of her other hand into my mouth to muffle my scream. She is not here to muffle me now.

I dry myself and snuggle into the bed, cradling my phone in the dark. Check Lex's account on Instagram, go too deep, and get careful to avoid any double taps, lest I give myself away. Here and there are shots of her, of us, of rooms and landscapes she took pictures of when I was not there. She could photograph the floor and make it look like an Eggleston. I wait to miss her more, but I feel blank, not quite new, but possible. I sleep hard, safe at last in the familiar landscape of my unconscious. The next morning, I wake as hung over by what I didn't drink as I've ever been by a bender. The sun is too bright. My chest too tight. My clothes smell old. But this tchotchke perdition offers solace: a new pair of jeans, a tshirt, cheap sandals from H&M. Amidst the labyrinthine and snaking walkways between hotels, the store is bound up with a Walgreens and a Margaritaville and a smattering of other eating and shopping establishments that have been smashed together like pieces of trash stuck by the river current between rocks. Supercuts trim. Drugstore sunglasses. A bag of Twizzlers and a cold Arizona Iced Tea. Maybe I should eat something better. Maybe I should go somewhere else. Cities can be like magnets that fling and draw you closer in turn. But I know that anywhere beyond here is terminal velocity—

leaving means who knows how long back to L.A., and L.A. still feels like the destination, even if the thought repels me further still.

I turn north towards Reno. As I spin away from Vegas, diminishing development and long stretches of nowhere extend from the dash of my Corolla. Every hundred miles or so, I get a wish to see Lex on the side of the road, hitchhiking. An alternate her, as haughty as Didion and as dgaf as Thompson, kicking at the dirt and on her way to Alaska. It is never she. She has become someone else. I text her: I'm alive. I'm sorry. I just need some time.

14

Lex heard from her mother that her father had died on a Wednesday evening, and I watched regret at a lost last chance for revenge pass across her face. It was right after I finally kicked my walking pneumonia, and we were at home, binge-watching David Attenborough-narrated nature everythings. She was quiet, and so I waited to be invited into her feeling. In the silence, a morass of grief and boundless hate grew in the room, chaotic and electric. I couldn't bring myself to move. We were stuck in the reality of a world without a monster, and it was without precedent in our lives.

I think I'm gonna head back into the office, she said, I really left a lot for tomorrow, and I continued sitting there, not knowing if I should grab her and hold her or let her go. I took the coward's choice. She called me later, said she'd left the lights on in the car and the battery was dead—could I come pick her up? Yeah, no problem, I said, and I fetched her because of course I would. Didn't get shit done, she said, as she closed the door. She folded her arms across her chest while I did my best to chauffeur stop at every light. She'd left her hoodie at her desk. Can we just drive a while? she asked. No problem, I said. I avoided the 10 and made my way down to Washington Boulevard, headed east and into the warehouse district. The sun was setting behind us and it cast long shadows across the windowless facades, offering up a gravel-lined version of minimalism most familiar to the folks working graveyard. She laid back and put her feet up and I turned on the heat to keep everything kosher as the desert cool whipped in the window. We did not talk.

After a while I noticed she was fingering the edge of her shirt in one hand, stemming over and over and over and watching the shadows become night. Past the industrial area, we ran into L.A. County's outer rim of communities, dotted by low-profile stucco houses with dirt and cactus yards. Teenagers parked their cars on the edge of the parking lot at Wal-Mart, their hoods up, and discussed transmissions, air intake, new timing belts. I drove slow enough to get a look at the mishmash of signage from the fifties, seventies, early aughts. The past didn't look as shiny as people pretend. Eventually Washington Ave dead-ended into a neighborhood of townhouses so I turned left up Whittier, towards the mountains. They could hardly be seen in the dark, but they loomed in front of us just the same. Let's go to that Taco Bell, Lex said, after we'd passed our second, and I obliged.

The day was gone. She ordered a steak quesarito and I wasn't ready to order, but then settled on a 7-layer burrito. We ate in a booth by the window. Not many other patrons around—couple of night workers on their way to the warehouses, a young het couple who seemed like they'd been together a while, and the employees, shooting the shit in between drive-thru orders. She said the quesarito was spicy and smirked. I mean, really spicy? I asked. She said no. White people spicy, she said. Like, I don't even know if you could eat this, she said and laughed. Then they definitely couldn't handle it in Portland, I said. No way, she said. They probably have quesarito challenges, she said. Like, how many bites can you take without sipping your Baja Fresh? I bet you could take a hundred, I said. At least, she said, and laughed. Winning would be the greatest badge of mediocrity, she said. As good as getting picked by the kiss cam at an NBA game.

For a few hours, again, she was the Lex of paint on her clothes and underground shows and too-late phone calls. Grief will do that, even good riddance grief, the kind that finalizes a rotten wish you're not allowed to say. The new person suit she'd taken to wearing slipped off. I was witness to the best of what she had been—ferocious and cocksure and without the noise of other people's reasons. It was selfish to prefer her this way, with the dead prole inside her kicked back from purgatory, but I didn't care. I stored the sight of her, laughing and sad with nacho cheese on her lips, right beside our past kisses and the way the Hudson sparkles at 3 a.m. Some things just don't get let go.

My bones had known I would probably leave before I knew it was possible. The theory was this: every relationship, every family, has a zenith, and the before and after of this point are just the ripples to and away from its brief perfection. My family was best when I was six, and only on Sunday evenings, when the routine of the week pulsed distractingly on the morning horizon. In the waning twilight we remained at rest and ready for what would come. When we grew older and my mother left and my father gave up, I wore those past evenings like strung jewels saved for future showoffs. See—here is when we were happy. Look how calm we are, how certain of who we could be. In the Boise Wal-Mart I wondered at which ripple I was in—the penultimate? the last?—and decided that Lex and I had peaked in the weeks just before our marriage, and our time since had been only a slow attenuated inertia. Here I stood alone, and numb.

I grabbed the Pert Plus and rounded the corner and there stood a woman, stouter and shorter and butcher, in western jeans and a blazer. She stared at the men's deodorants and I stared at her, and the bottom dropped out of me. I've never felt so needy. I wanted to rush her, hug her—get a good handshake-shake, maybe a hug and an eye-to-eye, so I could show off and be seen—but I did not know the secret lesbian morse code (if there was/is one anymore) and it was clear that my tomboy-femme-whatever could read as straight hipster woman as much as possible lezzi or bi. She didn't owe me her acknowledgment or care, anyway. I kept moving and went to home goods and bought a towel and then went back to toilet paper and cleaning products to grab some laundry detergent. We did not even make eye contact. She probably never saw me.

A sharp grief hid under my skin, like I might cry in the freezer section if I wasn't careful. At the checkout I focused on the other families and singletons and watched them as though I could understand what it was like to live in Idaho by proximity. The cashier was blonde, young, and wasn't much interested in making small talk. She had a nose piercing. The straight couple in front of me was buying three frozen pizzas, some cereal, milk, broccoli, artichokes, and various packages of shredded cheeses. He put mints on the belt as they got closer to the cashier. She put a trashy magazine she had been flipping through back on the rack. They looked like the last people under thirty and outside of Salt Lake City without tattoos. He had forward-gelled hair tips and one of those youth pastor goatees. She was trying for good wife. Who knew how close they were to the aisle. Neither had on rings. If they hadn't been standing in front of me, I wouldn't have even noticed them.

Goddamn it, Lex, you were the sun. The earth sprang from your mouth and the city (all cities?) did not exist until you showed them to me. Every morning belonged to you; I waited for your texts, and if I did not hear from you, I went through my day carrying your absence. When we reconnected I gave in, like I knew I shouldn't, because you were you, too real and the woman I had always wanted to love. But in Los Angeles, you forgot you ever lived in my country. Our proximity was not enough. We had become dream creatures to each other, reoccurring in the same scenes, familiar and strange. I picked up my groceries and followed the corral of people out the door.

It wasn't raining outside (why couldn't it at least be raining?) and I had been enough hours on the road that my rear end was sore and my posture needed a shoulder roll and wiggle to keep from seizing. I didn't call her, couldn't bring myself to say anything much to anyone, and stopped infrequently. Like a dumbshit, when I crossed the Oregon line, I realized where I was headed. I don't know that you can really drive without paying attention, but you can certainly head somewhere without noticing. As I hit The Dalles, the last three years hazed and sharpened in my memory. Technically I wanted to remember more togetherness, but I avoided the good moments to keep from turning around. Our marriage had been an accidental resolution, I told myself. The answer to an extended question. Yes, of course I love you. Yes, of course?

Bad pop on the radio. Tractor trailers going too fast or me going too slow. Black water to my right. I got tired. In the moonstruck night, rocks looked like doors you could walk through. Oncoming traffic metamorphed into trains passing. I took the next exit and pulled onto a side road, then another, and tucked myself in with my newly bought towel draped over me. About 4 a.m. I startled up shivering and headed out again, just to get the heater going.

The sun wasn't up yet, and I slapped my face to degrog. It had been a while since I'd been in the gorge. I knew that I knew how this piece of earth connected to the other places I have been, but I didn't much like the feeling. This was supposed to be the road out and away, but here I was going to the house again, like a goddamn salmon returning upstream to die.

We were all inside the house. My mother was mad about something—and James and I knew, intuitively, it had nothing to do with us. Our father, who even at his best could still be passively obnoxious—maybe he was to blame? He had never been good at conflict, but peace is worth little to the people holding their tongues to keep it. She didn't say she was mad, but she withdrew into a hard jaw and public solitude. No doubt she had ruminated in private, in her bedroom, in the bathroom, on long, solitary drives, but it was only the stiffness in the living room that I could witness. She did not frighten me when she was like this, but I also didn't want to get too close to her, as if I might accidentally fall into her orbit and disappear. James went over to his girlfriend's house. He didn't tell me, but I knew. I had tried cheering her up in the past, but she had snapped at me and I didn't have the temperament to try again.

Dad was out—running errands? Gran must've been sleeping. It was raining. I hid in my room. I liked how deep the colors seemed when it was gray outside, and I pulled out my Barbies to dress and style their hair. My friend Ariel, at school, had She-Ra action figures and American Girl dolls instead of Barbies because her mom had really intense ideas about role models, and I wished we had enough money for me to have toys like that too, but I also didn't mind my collection of different (but still the same?) characters from Mattel. It never occurred to me to want to be any of them. They were dolls.

One Ken. Six Barbies. Two off-brand dolls of the same size. Their names changed with their outfits. Mary Five, who lived at Five Five Five Fifth Avenue, was a recurring favorite, but the rest were a by-the-day selection of Kendras and Jessicas and Abbys and Ashleys and Melissas and whomever I imagined. Ken was Ken. I brushed

Abby's hair until it wasn't as knotted and then twisted it into the doll version of a chignon, as big as her head. For her outfit I chose a striped dress and decided to forgo the heels—they'd just fall off anyway. Her partner in crime I designated Christine and after trying a few mix and match pants and shirts, I settled on a long gown that was supposed to approximate evening-wear glamour. The long Velcro fastener down the back really took away from the classiness of the thing, but she looked as stunning as I could make her, and I set up my scene.

A pillowcase found, a few books borrowed. I turned the underside of a chair into the entrance of a theater. The pillowcase, folded into a thin line, was my (not) red carpet. Amidst my accessories I found a camera and put Christine in the center of the pillow, walking and waving to an imaginary audience as Abby snapped pictures of her. Christine! Christine! Abby shouted, but Christine couldn't be bothered. She was mugging for the other photographers. Abby didn't care. She got her shot, and then Christine disappeared behind the book walls of the theater entrance. Abby went to the windowsill, camera in hand, to take a few more shots, this time of the gray world outside. When she was done, she sat on the sill, her camera beside her, and wondered if any of them would turn out.

I changed her clothes and started over. Midway through a classroom mockup that I called college even though it more closely resembled my second-grade classroom, mom knocked on the door. Sweetie, she asked. I opened the door holding Ms. Mary Five, our dinosaur instructor. What are you doing? she asked. Playing Barbies, I said. She looked over my head at the mess on the floor. Can I play? she asked. I didn't really want her to, especially with her eyes all glassy and desperate, but she hadn't played with me in a long time. Sure, I said. She came in and sat cross-legged in her jeans, next to the scene I had set up. I sat across from her on the other side of the classroom. For seats, I had stacked books again, and sat the dolls two per book. In the front, a draped blanket over a chair set off the main classroom exhibit: an overly large stuffed brontosaurus. Ms. Mary Five had been discussing the controversy about brontosaurus skulls—had the wrong skull been placed on the skeleton? How can we know? And Ken kept interrupting her to ask if he could go to the bathroom.

Ms. Mary Five is teaching the class, I said. Mom picked up one of the classroom Barbies and brushed her hair. This one is scared of dinosaurs, she said. What's her name? I asked, and she did not know that this question was an offering. Her name is Molly, she said, and set her down. This one is Brenda, she said, and picked up a blonde from her bookseat. Brenda keeps interrupting, she said, Brenda doesn't know when to keep her mouth shut.

I put Ms. Mary Five back in the front of the classroom and Mary faced the class and said that for homework everyone had to draw a picture of an archaeopteryx. A what? mom asked. An arkey-op-trix, I said, it's an early bird ancestor. Where do you learn this stuff? she asked. From the library! I said. Look, I said, and I hopped up to grab the dinosaur encyclopedia I'd gotten the last time we visited. It felt weird and exciting to show mom what I liked doing, and she took the book from me with feigned interest. You always were a very curious kid, she said, and flipped through the pages, barely glancing at them before closing the book and saying she thought she should go lie down.

She got up and left me with my dolls and my dinosaurs. I didn't know why she, or I, should be so sad, but she made me want to cry. Her indifference clung to my book and my playtime and I abandoned them all to get under the covers of my bed and stare out the window. Someday I would leave and be able to have a home that felt full of whatever I wanted it to. Someday her naps and staring wouldn't be a part of my life anymore, and I'd thrill to read about dinosaurs and imagine a past without people. I just had to stay alive long enough to get there.

I was outside where the house should have been. No tattered hoodie sleeve to finger. No Leroy to hold hands with. There was new construction behind tarps behind scaffolding and a banner dropped over it all: Walgreens – Coming Soon!

The parking lot still smelled like tar, it was so freshly laid. Beside the tree where the head had rolled, the bushes had been removed, and the intersection itself had been expanded with dedicated turning lanes in each direction. No more confusion. No more accidents. There was no sidewalk, and where I stood was likely to become a landscaped buffer area where people might walk their dogs in a pinch, but it would be the only green surrounding an otherwise drab and predictable storefront. I didn't need to see it finished to know what it would look like.

It wouldn't look like the house. The house that I left, that I showed Lex, that reminded me why I moved away. It wouldn't look like the house we bathed in—me, James, mom, dad, gran—and ate and drank and slept and spent time in being bored, thinking we were waiting for our lives to start, unaware that they were already happening. Where James smashed Tonka trucks together and staged battles between superheroes and I organized my doll clothes into spring and winter collections. The house would not be quiet or loud, again, except in my memory of how silent the night could become, with the glow of our bedside lamps fanning under our doors into the hallways, the silence suddenly broken by the sound of James on the phone, loud and then hushed as he complained about who knows what to one of his long-forgotten girlfriends.

My home was gone, or maybe it had been gone, but at least now I knew it was gone, absolutely. I had not diaried there on my pilled blue bedspread in decades, and not one of us had avoided cutting the grass, paying off the neighbor's teenage son to do it on Sunday afternoon, us watching him *en masse* from the couches of our living room, with *The Poseidon Adventure* playing again on the USA network. We had all moved on. My mother had not missed this house, or the woman she had been in it—at least I thought, or believed? But what had I known, ever, of what she wanted. Our grandmother had died there and our father had built a better house (a jacuzzi tub in the master bath, they recently upgraded) with a better family in a better neighborhood in a worse town. Better by a standard that I neither wanted nor could be assessed against. Home ownership and family building were irrelevant to me, and now the house I had known and thought of as mine was a drugstore. I could not remember what color my bathroom had been. The traffic whirred, an unnatural tide behind me.

What was certain: our appliances were white, and the hook rug in the living room had been an accent piece (not wall to wall). The wicker hamper in the hall bathroom had slowly become gran's personal laundry dump, until she died, and then it had been used exclusively for towels. The vacuum had been stored in the coat closet by the front door for five years before finally being stuck next to the extra freezer in the garage. Three boxes of Christmas decorations in the attic never quite closed all the way so we started using black plastic bags to shield the garland from dust. I think mom's collection of spoons had been sold in a yard sale when I was a teenager, but I still remembered them hanging next to the breakfast table. So much was gone. The whys and hows and whats were fading. My most vivid memories had become like Christmas lights left on the roof long past the holiday, and it felt as though one more forgetting would darken them all.

Was it Ariel? Jen? who whooped me in Mario Kart, sitting cross-legged on the floor of the living room, and dad's friend Dave who would come over sometimes to help him clean out the gutters. Then they would stop and drink beer that had been stashed in the coolers they were sitting on and tell stories until the sun went down. The light rain fell on the roof. Mom would get gussied up and twirl in the hall and ask if she didn't look just like a party and then she'd disappear for the night and come back a little less coifed, a little more certain. Gran, shaking her head as she walked down the hall. Wouldn't you like a liverwurst sandwich? she would say, to request it for herself, sitting in her room as she watched *The Price Is Right*. There was a kewpie doll in the china cabinet, stashed behind the cordial glasses we never used. Doilies over the worn orange-and-yellow plaid fabric of the easy chair. We ate dinner at the breakfast table and never in the dining room.

I walked to where the head had been and the head was not there, the same as the house was not here, but I was in what had been the yard, as I had been before. Michael was in Texas and could not get V away from there. James was in Denver and not smoking weed in his room. Sharon wasn't yelling at me to come inside. I was grown and there was no showing where or what went into me from the first, before I knew I would care that it had. We were what was left, and we were scattered from where we started.

When Lex and I were smashing back together, when I had turned the fade on the old man, Lex told me a story about her and her mom that I had loved then, because I had loved her, even though I had not really understood it until later. She had been happy when she told it and we were at Marshall Stack and she was nursing a martini. Mom, she started, mom couldn't afford most of what Bloomingdales even sells, but she'd pop in sometimes to buy a lipstick and I'd get to tag along. We'd get soup in the café and then we'd pretend like we were rich and browse the ladies separates and women's handbags. I knew we couldn't buy anything, but I'd watch the other, taller women as they went—why were they always taller? she laughed—and they'd scroll through hangers looking for their size or picking up a sleeve to examine the fabric. It made me so mad that they could buy things we couldn't, she said.

Rightly so, I said, it's so arbitrary—who ends up with how much. But I can buy that stuff now, she said. It's what I want. I've always wanted to be able to live like that. She had sipped her martini and set it down again, fingering the toothpick and olive balanced precariously inside. I remember being in awe of her, how sure and stalwart she had become. Just beyond her a thin white woman entered the bar, clutching her yoga mat like a life raft. She scanned the room for someone she knew and then darted to a man in a Yankees cap nursing a beer by the back wall. He glanced at the game on the television as he hugged her. Lex touched my leg and brought me back to her, scooting to the edge of her stool until our knees folded together. I parted my lips. She touched them with her outstretched thumb and rubbed as if smearing lipstick that wasn't there. You look so surprised with your mouth open, she said. And I had blushed.

We didn't talk for longer than I expected. Maybe it was the too-closeness of us over the years that made me expect otherwise, but in my fleeing, we allowed each other the silence. I made it to Portland in one piece and told no one I was there. Stayed at cheap hotels and bounced between a few coffee haunts I used to sit in over a decade before. Drove the streets, marveling at all the new buildings that had been built, the street names that had changed, the gas stations that had been torn down. The Egyptian Room was long gone. Halcyon was still there, but the kids were younger or I was older or both. No more Fez. Powell's still. Hung Far Low had its signage but the restaurant was permanently closed. Everything seemed a little shinier, a little newer, a little more cramped. Cars were everywhere in stop and go hell. I didn't recognize the city of my youth. There were no hand-holds to grab, no one to call on the phone.

In the evenings I flipped through the Gideon Bible in my motel room, asking it questions and picking passages at random like a magic eight ball. Question: Is it over with Lex? *I call with all my heart. Answer me, O Lord, and I will obey your decrees.* Question: Should I get revaccinated for tetanus? *Man's days are determined; you have decreed the number of his months and set limits he cannot exceed.* (UM) Question: Will coffee really go extinct? *Peter took him aside and began to rebuke him. Never, Lord! he said. This shall never happen to you.* Question again: Is it over with Lex? *These double calamities have come upon you—who can comfort you?—ruin and destruction, famine and sword—who can console you?* I put it back in the drawer and turned on Animal Planet to watch some puppies, but instead I landed on some horrific cat surgery. Bounced away and stuck with a face cream infomercial where the woman praising the cream's effects clearly didn't get the dregs of the genetic lottery. I wondered about who believes this stuff, and then remembered how many bathrooms I've been in that are temples of self-hate. So much bullshit to live with. When I got the first impulse to call Lex and try and explain myself, I still didn't. Pride? Shame? Same-same. I knew I would probably say I missed her, but I didn't want her to know how fucked up I was, at least not from my own mouth.

I email work and apologize for not showing up; write one version that says I'll be back by Monday. The one I actually send says thank you for the opportunity, but I won't be returning for the foreseeable future. They write back an hour later saying my departure is unexpected but they wish me the best. Turns out it doesn't take much to get further from the city, with fewer reasons to return. I change the channel. And again. And again and again and again and again.

15

When I was thirteen I snuck into a half-finished stucco house that had been left on the market too long and its emptiness had begun to pervade the wood studs and poured concrete the way that spirits sometimes stay near their graves. The dining room window hadn't been locked shut and so I just lifted it and crawled inside and Sarah was with me and Trina wasn't in the picture yet and so I was excited. We split up and walked around, opening cabinets and picking up tools that had been left lying around. Whenever we heard a car, we'd stop dead in our tracks to listen and see if someone was coming to the house, but they never were. When I was in the kitchen, Sarah came up behind me and tapped my shoulder and screamed tag! you're it! and so I chased her and then tagged her and then she chased me and tagged me until we had been in every room and up the stairs and then the last time she grabbed me and we wrestled onto the floor, laughing and panting, and she was on top of me and then I was on top of her and then we were side by side, holding hands, saying hellooooo with our voices echoing off the empty walls. I knew then that I loved her without knowing what that meant, just that I liked being in the world with her, and I liked it best when we could be alone.

When we left the house it was drizzling, and so we ran back to my house and I took the first shower and she took the second and then she borrowed some of my clothes to wear for the afternoon. We listened to CDs on my boombox and James came in and asked if we'd seen dad—it must've been a Saturday—and we said no, but mom was in the kitchen, and then he disappeared again. Mom made us leave the door open, which I thought was weird, but whatever, and then we got out scissors and glue and a big stack of magazines and made collages of pretty women and chopped up ad slogans gluestick-pasted onto construction paper backgrounds. I called mine The Book of Model Memories and she called hers Trash Art and then mom said Sarah's mom was there to pick her up and so we hugged each other, and then we said goodbye and I picked a piece of lint off her shirt and she said thanks and then waved bye and we said bye like we always did, as friends.

I left Lex, and I'm still no good at goodbyes. I cried across Kansas and cursed my way through Missouri and called her as I drove into St. Louis. The words I was afraid to say, I said, and she didn't say much at first, and then said she thought this might be coming. She asked when I'd get my stuff, asked about papers, wondered why now, offhand said we should have never gotten married, said things how people do when they are saying what they think they should say. I did not answer, did not know any logistics, and then I said I'll email you, and she said don't call until you know better what you're going to do, and I got mad and then we stayed on the phone too long. I don't know what she did right after. I got a motel room and then went to BB's and listened to the blues. I ate wings, alone, and hated that I was relieved. I wanted her even as I left her, but I knew I needed different to live. The beginning of the end was done.

In the flat and lonely land of southern Illinois the sky rose up over the land like I could see the dome of the earth if I just squinted at the horizon. When an exit came I pulled off the interstate and took a no-name road to another no-name intersection and got out and watched a combine pass, taller than two of my Corollas stacked on top of each other. Amidst the light cerulean above me, bulbous clouds dotted the sky and I wondered about Jay, and where near here she had grown up.

Did she know these streets the same as I knew Hobart and 99E? Had she, in her brief and close love of Lex, uncovered something that I could never? It was as if we knew something essential about each other, because we had both kissed Lex. Both of us, and the people we knew, and the people we didn't know we knew, were tangled across states and between destinations, our footsteps and bodies flung across this odd and genocidal country—so many entrances and exits, mistakes and possibilities. What extinct creatures had also stepped or swum here? What families had passed through or stayed, worked and laughed where I now stood? The Winnebego? Kickapoo? I didn't know enough to say, and I was ashamed. Jay came from near here, that's all I had, and I was passing through. More traffic. I got back on the road and drove parallel to the interstate for as long as I could, but the hours made me anxious to arrive somewhere, and soon I was back in the midst of the other travelers. I forget now, how I survived it, but I did.

Do you ever wake up and feel like you would swarm if you could? I asked Leroy, after we are assembled in the living room with my clothes tossed in the corner. I am lounging in a borrowed robe, like I do in this place, with his fresh soap smell on my skin from a desperate and necessary shower. Like bees? he said. Yeah, like I feel like a swarm, I said. Slowly he smoked the spliff between his thumb and forefinger, his feet propped on the coffee table.

Maybe you were a hornet in another life, he said. And you? I asked. A copperhead, he said, couldn't you tell? I said I should have known and leaned back on the couch and stared at the stipple ceiling. The light on the mottling danced and I thought I could see waves in it if I watched closely enough. This only weed and tobacco? I asked. Yeah, he said. Good shit, I said. We laughed, not because it was funny, but because we were in love.

The room smelled sour, a little like too much work and the things we do after work to forget. I didn't mind. I was high as fuck and safe beside the only person who knew which questions were worth asking and when it wasn't worth pushing for more. Jeremy came in when we were in the middle of a good diss on Portland. He'd gained a little weight since last I saw him and had that fresh swagger that gets into people who are good and loved. Hey stranger, I said, and got up and we slapped hands as if it was something we always did. How's my favorite night urchin? he asked, and I said I'd been better. He said he'd heard, and I said at least I know that I'm the problem. Aren't we all? he laughed and went to the kitchen for a beer. Me, the problem. Us, other people's problems.

They let me drive anyway, the next day, when we went out in my Corolla to the city or downtown or whatever Asheville qualifies for, so hilly and unevenly assembled amidst the wooden and near mountains. We walked around and popped into shops to look at clothes and dishes and art we couldn't buy and then we splurged and got a late lunch at Tupelo Honey Café.

Jeremy ate his peas with syrup strung along the edge of his knife and Leroy grinned at him as he exaggerated the motion against his tongue. When we were done, Jeremy said the meal would do him for the late shift and Leroy said Jeremy'd gotten a new job over at the Building Materials center on the edge of town. You're still at the hotel, though, right? I asked, and Leroy said he was, but lucky for him he was on a more usual schedule these days, Monday through Friday. I haven't asked, he started, and I said I'd quit my job on the way out. Via email. No notice. Sometimes you gotta run for a while, he said, and I raised my lemonade in agreement. He didn't ask me where-to or what-for. When I'd told him about me and Lex after showing up, unannounced, he'd said come in and given me a hug and I had cried a little, and that was that.

On the drive home it was evening and we were on a curvy road behind a big SUV and Leroy was talking about Lacan and *RuPaul's Drag Race* and the tension of symbolic gender destruction and affirmation through drag and suddenly in front of us was a dead deer, a WHOLE dead deer in the center of the road and we hadn't seen it before and I couldn't swerve because a car was coming the other way and the other side of the road dropped off into a valley beside me and so I squared up and we screamed AGHHHH and then we hit the deer full-on. It knocked against the bottom of the car in sick and morbid drumming. In the rearview mirror I saw a leg swing up as the deer emerged horrific and in more pieces behind us and we kept going and exhaled and said omg ten times I can't believe that just happened. We're all okay, aren't we? We're all okay. Back at the parking lot at their duplex we got down on our stomachs and looked for any major damage, and everything looked fine, with a few tufts of brown here and there stuck to the pipes. Even if it had been a straightaway I probably couldn't have swerved, I said, because I knew a wheel stuck in the belly of a deer would be no good for anyone's forward trajectory. You did the right thing, said Jeremy, and we all went inside.

The thought of Florida occurred to me. Some dilapidated place that was salt and sun bleached like the negative of its former self, framed in cracking concrete and pastel paint. Maybe Destin—destinies, floridays, meth, a shark bite, hours diving into waves, sand in my car, working retail. I could flirt with skin cancer, cultivate an opinion about rum. But I wasn't self-destructive enough. Leroy said if I drove south he'd burn an effigy and I knew better than to compound my own addiction to novelty with his mountain curses.

Lex got a new wife after I got my stuff. I cut my hair, sold my Corolla and bought an even older truck. Drove up to New York to visit my women and Cecilia cried when we finally met up. She said she'd been so worried about me. I haven't heard from you in months, she said, and I said I was sorry. I needed to be alone, I said, away from everything, when what I meant was away from anything and anyone that reminded me of Lex, of our life together, and what we once had. How's Trish? I asked and she said she'd moved down to Atlanta—got a big editing job at Turner. But Cora's still here. Still at Condé. Haven't heard from Yvonne lately, tbh. Been too busy to get back to Cubby much, she said. I've been doing a weekly mix show on this radio station that broadcasts on the web. I smiled and said it was nice to be back in New York. You staying? she asked, and I asked if I could crash for a little while, and she said I was good for a month and then I had to pay rent. I said it wouldn't be that long, and then she hugged me like she didn't want me to die. I'm alright, I lied. I said it again when I met up with Claire for drinks in Long Island City. She ordered a Manhattan. I ordered a Long Island Ice Tea. We laughed at ourselves and when I told her I was alright I said it like I might believe it, and then I said it again like I knew it was true. On the phone I said it to my dad like I was dusting dirt off my pants, and to Leroy, who checked in a little more than usual, I said it quiet, like a child. I'm alright. I'll be alright.

It wasn't Lex's fault, or at least it wasn't more her fault than mine. She wanted a good plus one, and I had discovered (almost too late) that I was no good at wanting the same thing. It didn't mean I didn't love her. I knowingly snapped myself in half to not go back. I chose my pain. When I told her I wanted a divorce, she said why, and I said I didn't think it mattered why. It mattered that I had said I was done. In New York I cried myself to sleep on Cecilia's couch and quieted myself when I heard Cora come in. I cried other nights, unexpected, and slept and got up and lived half a day, then another. At first I thought time had reset, that I was back in the city with nothing to comfort me, but my second itinerancy was heavy with grief. I missed the stars. Every subway delay felt personal. When a man catcalled me at Columbus Circle, I turned and walked towards him screaming WOULD YOU LIKE TO SAY IT AGAIN? until he ran off into the park and I slumped on the concrete, wail-crying my frustration and sadness. An old woman offered me her hand. Get up, she said. It's too cold to cry here.

We were all inside the house (now gone) and James was meditating in his room. Gran was taking a nap and mom was watching tv in the living room. Dad was in the garage, putting up a pegboard so he could organize the yard tools. I snuck from room to room, slowly opening drawers I wasn't really supposed to look in. In mom and dad's bathroom I found tubes of BenGay and Desitin and Vagisil and wondered how or why a person could need so many different creams. A white candle rolling around, with the bottom worn down on the side. Partially used packs of Kleenex and random hair ties that mom had kleptoed from me over time. An opened box of qtips, stashed tampons and maxipads, an electric hair clipper and its different attachments. In their bedroom, the bottom drawer of the dresser was stuffed with socks, matched and mismatched. Mostly black for dad. Stripes and whites and multicolored patterns for mom. Behind the socks I found a grocery bag with letters dad had written mom before they were married. The bag was loud and so I opened it carefully and pulled out one of the letters to read. I scanned it quickly. Lot of I miss yous. Then this from dad: mom says I should wait for a college girl—I told her college was no guarantee of smarts.

I heard someone coming. I folded the letter up and stuffed it back in the envelope and gently hid the stack again behind the socks. Closed the drawer. Promised myself I'd go back and read it again, read the rest, but I didn't. Time took over. Distraction.

It was gran who I had heard. She shuffled by and joined mom in the living room to watch tv. Some Rogers and Hammerstein musical—*Oklahoma*? *Showboat*? (I pretended to like them because I thought it was polite.) I snuck down to my room and got out my journal—rarely used—and waited. Nothing felt worth writing down. Men's voices sang from the other room. Dad came in from the garage and went to take a shower. James opened the door to his room and passed by on his way to the kitchen, probably to get a snack. We were all inside the house, alone.

When I picked up my stuff from California I kept a suitcase worth of clothes and the raccoon skull from western Carolina. The other skulls I put in the dumpster, along with most of my toiletries and collected mementos: concert tickets, amateur pottery, notes and unused stationary, aspirational pants. She kept the furniture. She kept whatever I didn't remark on, touch. I thought I got everything I cared about, but the other day she posted a picture of her wife in a pair of jeans I left behind. I didn't expect her to remember whose was whose, what was artifact, what was thing, but it surprised me and I wondered what other scraps of mine still floated in and out of her life. It isn't that I wanted her to keep my spot blank, if wife could be said to have been my spot for any time at all (her new wife was more beautiful), but I expected more finality, an end.

She said I looked tired while I packed, that I looked distracted, and I said I guess I've had a lot on my mind. I remember it was hot when I got to the apartment and the neighborhood didn't look the same. A new hotpot restaurant had opened up. The usual cars were a little shuffled, a little different, and I noticed this change with the same antenna vibration that knows the night sky is unfamiliar in other latitudes. She wanted to hear where I was crashing, and I said I was staying with Cecilia for now. She said Cecilia was a good egg and she sat down and she watched me while I went through the closets, went back and forth to the dumpster. She had expelled our life before I left and I was tardy, as I had been so often to school. Later I found out she was already dating the woman she would marry only months after I left, which explained the phone placed close to her hand, just in case. Their love affair was no doubt torrid. Late-night waking on Saturdays and surprise flowers from the supermarket. This new wife's future may follow and proceed from the life I lived, but I do not care to know more of it than what accidentally crosses my various feeds. Her name is irrelevant. I've already spent too much time imagining it.

After I left I cried so much I forgot what my eyes looked like when I was young. She called me when she was sad and I said I couldn't make it better. I couldn't undo what I had done. And then I hung up and cried some more.

In New York I avoided the news, skipped over political posts on facebook (so much of the same horrors—was it Russians? was it us? yes) woke, walked, slept in a different spin. Imagined kids in border concentration camps imagining safety away from where they were. Hoped for people who would help; knew I should be one of them, felt guilty, didn't change. I embodied impotence. Scrolled through Instagram. Was a joke, but clung to my grief. The usual consumption—Reese's Pieces, gin, books, ebay—improved nothing. Work came and went: gig economy bullshit. Tech maxims and marketing lies. We are all unequal; some of us are more unequal than others.

The city was too shiny, full of false life. Bars packed with men that looked like Brett Easton Ellis in a circle jerk calling each other Brett. I temped and languished and left work with anger, spat, looked for graffiti, avoided silver escalators and retreated to Coney Island. Walked the boardwalk at night and went out on the pier, weaving between the Chinese men catching crabs with chicken on strings. I wanted their crabs. I wanted their knowledge, their courage, their world-away from what they had known. I stared at the ferris wheel and listened to the waves. I came back on the weekends and watched the Black Brooklyn families and Russian men in the sand, getting too hot in the sun, jumping into the water, avoiding the trash, avoiding the white bicyclists, spending time like time was easy, like summers were long. I listened for children. I wondered how I would pay Cecilia.

New York might have had my answers before I ever showed up, but I'd been there and back again enough to know I was looking for a city that hadn't existed for a long time. I borrowed cash from my dad, plus an extra three thousand to leave. Told Cecilia I had to go. Dad asked where I was going and I said somewhere small. He said I could come to Lufkin and I said I think I need a colder winter. The truck was still kicking and I didn't have much baggage to show for my attempt at making the city home again. It was just as well; it (or I) hadn't lasted. I set the raccoon skull on the dash and headed due west on I-78 Other people went north and dug into upstate, but I wanted bigger sky. Moving was enough for the present. The skull rattled as I left my friends and familiar options behind.

The problem is I know how it all ends, in blood and quiet, and I learned that final lesson when I was too young to know what was routine and what was unusual, and how everyone mixes up the two. The dead leave us with trash to pick up and hide. They leave us sinew and flesh, soon to rot, and they leave us wrecked in our own homes, as full of emptiness as they ever were with noise. The living leave a different absence. Shadows and holograms full of possible rekindling. Hearts burnt to charcoal, waiting for a reason to flame.

The plants are growing in the sill and it will be summer soon. I stir cream into my coffee. This apartment has a way of feeling empty even when it's occupied, and I like the stillness of it, broken up in small chaos by Edgar and Jim—my cat and dog, respectively. It turns out I prefer the company of animals. Chicago suits me, plopped in the middle of everywhere. It isn't small, like I thought I was looking for, but it is vital and pulsing and violent. When I first arrived, last fall, I wiggled into my corner of the Gold Coast with stubborn determination and secured employment: another desk with another phone and another executive to pander to. The life of a secretary. And the familiar shield of irrelevance settled around me.

I didn't leave the apartment much, at first, because the cold was hard on my new skin, and now I haven't left much during the spring either, because the pandemic has kept me—us—home. Jim has become accustomed to pee pads in the kitchen. My new job has become a remote desktop connection. A feigned happiness on the phone. Be grateful to the wind, I tell myself, and then I bake to stay sane. Muffins, rolls, bread, pizza dough, casseroles, chicken thighs, cakes, pies, quiche, an attempted soufflé. Catch up with Leroy on the phone. Scope out the usual dating apps, but it seems futile; there is nowhere to go. Besides I can't remember how to care. How to believe someone's face on whatever app could ever become important to me. The bread is delicious.

When I shower and dress I study my face, with the skull more prominent, and the lines around my eyes hinting at an uncertain future, and I remember Portland, and New York, and Los Angeles, and their memory feels as different and far from this new reality as if I have left a continent behind. Lex's mother has come down with Covid (I saw on facebook) and there's nothing I can say. That's also what time has done. Her mom was family to me, and now she's someone I have no reason to talk to. We are estranged by time, by choice.

When I hear the traffic and the birds sing at sunrise, it occurs to me that my clean bathroom and well-placed rugs are as much my companions as Edgar, as Jim. I stare at the wall and remember the blood on Lex's face and the stare of that unknown woman as she died in my yard as a kid, and I remember what I didn't ever want to know about mom's final minutes and the loneliness that has been my truest friend, and then I spiral into other memories: the feeling of naked skin against mine at 3 a.m. with a throbbing buzz behind my eyes, the flavor of Lex's skin on my tongue and the lips of the old man, and these are mine too, as present and loved as the woven rags under my feet. Then as now, now as then.

Mom told me we were all inside the house. Even her mother, Margot, was there (she died a year later—breast cancer or the treatment is what they said), and gran and dad and James. Somewhere on the Lower East Side Lex was sitting in a high chair while her abuela fed her mashed bananas, but I didn't know any of that then. I didn't know much at all because I was a baby, my head flaccid and wobbling when any of them forgot to hold it. Mom told me they were all sitting in the living room and passing me around the room and cooing and talking about how much I looked like dad and how much I looked like mom and look at those big brown eyes and she's a good healthy size for sure.

When the game came on (was it New Years? Or Thanksgiving?) they handed me to mom and I cried then screamed then sobbed. They looked at her like she should do something, like I should fix it, fix YOU, she told me, and she held me and bobbed me up and down and I caught my breath and screamed some more. She took me in the back room, to the bedroom she shared with dad, and she says she walked around and pointed at things outside to distract me and set me down (but I wanted to be held) and tried toys and socks and jewelry and her own breast and still I cried. She checked my diaper and patted my back, but I cried into halftime and after, when dad came in and said oh Sharon, lemme try, and she said okay, but I wouldn't stop, not when he held me, not when she took me back. I cried until I couldn't catch my breath, and then I cried some more, and then, when she had begun to wonder if it was possible for a baby to die of crying, I stopped. You never cried like that again, she told me. But I was always afraid you would.

Lex posts a picture of her and her wife on instagram. She looks great (of course she looks great) and content and that's what I want for her. Her hair is a little longer, tucked behind her ears in a sharp bob that draws more attention to her jawline. The wife is to her left, my right, and they are trying at optimism, putting on the mask of strength that we all attempt when we gather online now. No one knows what will come.

I double-tap. Edgar hops on the table and I run my hand through his fur. My coffee needs a refresh and I should take Jim for a walk. Maybe later. The sheets need changing. I put down my phone and open a window to let in the breeze. Sunlight skips along the rug and Edgar jumps down to catch it. Jim follows me to the bedroom and nestles into the dirty sheets I strip from the bed. I pull the fitted sheet to each corner, and tuck the top sheet under the foot, to make almost-hospital corners like my mother taught me. Smooth the comforter on top. Re-sheathe and fluff the pillows. I love my room. Quiet and cheerful like you wouldn't believe.

It's enough.

Acknowledgments

First: I am grateful to Tye, my great love, and the most interesting person I know. I love you throughout time.

Second: I am grateful to Alan Good, my editor and founder of this dang press. There are a lot of editors out there who do harm—to authors, to their work, to our culture, to the reputation of publishing, hell, to humanity. Alan isn't one of them, and I'm grateful to be read, edited, and published by him.

Third: I am grateful to Linda Pierce, whose generosity has changed my life numerous times, and whose wit is so sharp and lingering, it makes me smile even when we are apart.

Fourth: I am grateful to Donald, who knows all my secrets.

Fifth: I am grateful to Vic and Anjuli, Britt, Sarah, Marina, Syd, Renee, Mary, Renee, and Daniel, for your friendship, and for helping me see who I was when I most needed to open my eyes.

Sixth: I am grateful to Beverly, champion of the good life and my dear friend, who read an early draft and encouraged me to continue.

Seventh: I am grateful to Carmen and Ephraim, and the rest of the AllofUs crew, because you know every bend in the road.

Eighth: I am grateful to Hannah, my handsome and beautiful sister, who taught me how to be brave.

Ninth: I am grateful for the friends, lovers, instructors, and family whose influence made me into the person who wrote this book. I love you, and I hope you know who you are.

Lastly: I am grateful to you, dear reader, for supporting an independent press, reading independent authors, and offering me your time and attention.

LJ Pemberton is a writer/artist whose essays, poetry, and award-winning stories have been featured in *The Baffler*, *Los Angeles Review*, *Exacting Clam*, *PANK*, *Malarkey Books*, *Brooklyn Rail*, *Electric Encyclopedia of Experimental Literature*, *Northwest Review*, and elsewhere. She holds an MFA from Columbia University and a BA from Reed College. This is her first novel.

Find out more at ljpemberton.com.

Other Titles from Malarkey Books

Faith, a novel by Itoro Bassey
The Life of the Party Is Harder to Find Until You're the Last One Around, poems by Adrian Sobol
Music Is Over, a novel by Ben Arzate
Toadstones, stories by Eric Williams
Deliver Thy Pigs, a novel by Joey Hedger
It Came From the Swamp, edited by Joey Poole
Pontoon, an anthology of fiction and poetry
What I Thought of Ain't Funny, an anthology of stories based on the jokes of Mitch Hedberg, edited by Caroljean Gavin
Guess What's Different, essays by Susan Triemert
White People on Vacation, a novel by Alex Miller
Your Favorite Poet, poems by Leigh Chadwick,
Sophomore Slump, poems by Leigh Chadwick
Man in a Cage, a novel by Patrick Nevins
Fearless, a novel by Benjamin Warner
Don Bronco's (Working Title) Shell, a novel? by Donald Ryan
Un-ruined, a novel by Roger Vaillancourt
Thunder From a Clear Blue Sky, a novel by Justin Bryant
Kill Radio, a novel by Lauren Bolger
The Muu-Antiques, a novel by Shome Dasgupta
Backmask, a novel by OF Cieri
Gloria Patri, a novel by Austin Ross
Where the Pavement Turns to Sand, stories by Sheldon Birnie

Thumbsucker, poems by Kat Giordano
Hope and Wild Panic, stories by Sean Ennis
Sleep Decades, stories by Israel A. Bonilla
I Blame Myself But Also You (and Other Stories),
by Spencer Fleury
The Great Atlantic Highway & Other Stories,
by Steve Gergley
First Aid for Choking Victims,
stories by Matthew Zanoni Müller

malarkeybooks.com

www.ingramcontent.com/pod-product-compliance
Lightning Source LLC
LaVergne TN
LVHW042250040525
810388LV00028B/427